"You should go inside."

"Why?" Jessica forced herself to look away from Cooper, to gaze out into the featureless night. "It's beautiful out here. The weather's perfect—"

"I'm not talking about the weather."

She turned back to look at Cooper. She had no choice. The darkness in his voice drew her. "I'm not afraid of you," she murmured.

"You should be."

She took a step toward him. One small step. But it was enough. Enough to touch him. Enough to let him know he'd have to be the one to walk away. She wasn't about to make it easy on him. "What could one night together hurt?"

"You don't know what you're asking."

"Yes. I do." She wanted to hold him, to absorb the danger and excitement that was Sam Cooper. For once in her life, she wanted to do the unexpected. She wanted the forbidden. She looked into his eyes and whispered, "Just one night, Cooper. That's all I'm asking."

Dear Reader,

Ever since Sam Cooper first waltzed onto the pages
of *Keeping Katie,* my first Harlequin Superromance
novel, I've wanted to tell his story. I hadn't planned on
him, he just appeared one day, a bold, brash, sexy
private investigator who stood toe-to-toe with my
hero, Alan Parks.

Cooper was the perfect Temptation hero, a real rogue,
and from the start I knew he was a loner. But even then,
I could see another side to him, a softer side. I believed
that all he needed to bring it out was the right woman.
That's where Jessie Burkett comes in, a woman as
strong and determined as Cooper himself, with a
capacity for love that not even a loner can resist.

So my first Temptation novel was born, with a hero to
die for and a woman who makes him care. For all those
readers who wrote asking for Cooper's story, here it is.
I hope you enjoy it.

Patricia Keelyn

Books by Patricia Keelyn

HARLEQUIN SUPERROMANCE
590—KEEPING KATIE
631—WHERE THE HEART IS
682—ONCE A WIFE

Don't miss any of our special offers. Write to us at the
following address for information on our newest releases.

Harlequin Reader Service
U.S.: 3010 Walden Ave., P.O. Box 1325, Buffalo, NY 14269
Canadian: P.O. Box 609, Fort Erie, Ont. L2A 5X3

NOBODY'S
HERO
Patricia Keelyn

Harlequin Books

TORONTO • NEW YORK • LONDON
AMSTERDAM • PARIS • SYDNEY • HAMBURG
STOCKHOLM • ATHENS • TOKYO • MILAN
MADRID • WARSAW • BUDAPEST • AUCKLAND

For Melissa Beck, Susan Goggins,
Carol Springston and Lynn Styles,
who helped me create KK.
I couldn't give you that one,
so I thought it fitting that you should have
Cooper's story.

ISBN 0-373-25682-5

NOBODY'S HERO

Printed in U.S.A.

Prologue

NICOLE THOUGHT FIRST of Jessie.

Racing through her dark house, grateful for the cold, silent marble floors beneath her bare feet, Nicole worried about her sister. About Jessie. About what it would do to her when Nicole turned up dead.

On the stairs she moved slower, listening to see if they'd followed her yet, knowing not even the marble could mask the sounds of booted feet.

Nothing.

She hurried on, slipping into the safety of her suite, her sanctuary, and locking the door behind her. Leaning against it, she pressed her ear to the hard wood, listening. She heard only her own wildly beating heart and heavy breathing. No one had followed her. She was safe.

For the moment.

But the suite wouldn't shelter her for long. Not even Robert could protect her now. She knew too much. She'd seen the Colonel's face. It was as simple as that.

Panic fluttered through her.

Moving to her desk, Nicole picked up the phone and dialed the number she knew by heart. Jessie would know what to do. But when her sister answered, Nicole couldn't speak. She couldn't draw Jessie into this.

"Hello," Jessie said again. "Is anyone there?"

Two loud knocks sounded on the door.

Nicole froze, then hung up the phone as quietly as possible. When the knock came again, louder this time, fear washed over her like a cresting wave.

"Nicki!" Robert demanded. "Let me in."

Frantically, she glanced around the sitting room. There were only two other ways out—through her bedroom, or through the double French doors that opened onto the second-floor veranda. She dismissed her bedroom immediately; it led back to the hall where they waited for her. That left the veranda and a long drop to a concrete patio.

"Nicole!"

At the commanding tone, she froze. It was the cold, menacing voice she'd heard in her husband's study earlier tonight. The voice she wished she'd never heard. Never recognized.

"Nicole!" he said again. "Open the goddamn door!"

The veranda was her only chance. Because if she waited until they broke down her door, she'd have no chance at all.

1

WHENEVER TROUBLE FOUND him, it appeared in the form of a woman. He didn't know what drew them to him or why they always spelled disaster. But from the looks of things, this time was no exception.

He'd noticed her the moment she'd set foot in the marina, and the uneasy feeling that hit him in the gut predicted problems. She wore jeans and a dark, long sleeved blouse, and she looked as out of place in the Fort Lauderdale heat as snow in Miami. But she wasn't a tourist figuring to rent a fishing boat for the day. This woman wanted something else entirely, and he didn't want to know what.

He'd watched her walk up and down the docks, scanning the boats. Then she'd spotted the *Freedom Chaser* and headed straight for him. And for once he wished his instincts had been wrong.

He continued varnishing the teak trim as she approached, not bothering to look up even when she stopped on the dock beside his boat.

"You're not an easy man to find," she said, in a voice as deep and dusky as a moonless night.

He kept his attention on his work. "I like it that way."

"Don't you ever check your answering machine? Or return your calls?"

Her voice disturbed him. Almost as much as her presence. "Sometimes."

"Sometimes?" She hesitated, and he guessed his answer wasn't to her liking. "That seems like a hell of a way to run a business."

Without standing, he shifted to look up at her for the first time. She stood with her back to the sun, so he couldn't make out her features, but it didn't matter. He didn't know her. Didn't care to, despite the way those jeans snugly clung to her long, slender legs, or the way her voice sent waves of pleasure down his spine.

"You *are* Sam Cooper," she stated, obviously uncomfortable with his scrutiny and his silence. "The private investigator." She made it sound like "the serial killer."

He returned to his varnishing, touching up a spot here, evening out a streak there. "Yeah."

"I've been trying to reach you for days." Then, when he didn't respond, she added, "I'm Jessica Burkett. Jacob Anderson sent me."

"Figures."

"You've talked to Jacob?"

"Nope. But there aren't a whole lot of people who know where to find me." He set the brush into a nearby pan of turpentine and, wiping his hands on a rag, stood and faced the woman who'd invaded his sanctuary. He could tell he wasn't going to get much else done until he'd sent her on her way. "Fewer still who'd have the nerve to send someone after me."

Now that he'd risen to her level, he could see her better. She was a small woman, delicately boned, with a short cap of dark, wavy hair. She struck him as a bundle of barely contained energy within a pixie-cute package. But something in her large eyes told him she wouldn't appreciate being called cute. How like Anderson to bait the hook with a pretty woman.

But Cooper wasn't biting. Not this time.

"I'm afraid you've wasted a trip, Ms. Burkett." Anderson might know his weaknesses, but it wasn't going to work. "Now run on back to Chicago and tell your boss I'm not interested."

"My boss?" She crossed her arms, evidently in no hurry to respond to his dismissal.

"Jacob Anderson. Tell him I'm on vacation."

"I don't work for Jacob."

Somehow Cooper doubted the truth of that, but he remained silent.

"He told me where to find you," she continued, "because I want to hire you myself."

"Well then, I'm doubly sorry you've wasted your time. As I said, I'm on vacation."

"I can pay you."

Cooper let out a short laugh. "I doubt you can afford me. And even if you could, I don't do private work."

She looked confused, and Cooper silently cursed Anderson once again. "I don't work for individuals," he explained, wondering why he bothered. He didn't owe this woman anything. But he spelled it out anyway. "I don't work for people with more at stake than money."

"How nice for you."

He suppressed the urge to defend his position. Again he reminded himself that he didn't owe her anything. He started to turn away, but stopped when she said, "Mr. Cooper, I've traveled fifteen hundred miles to find my sister and then spent two days tracking you down. The least you can do is hear me out."

"It's just plain Cooper, ma'am. And as I said, I don't do private work." This time he succeeded in turning back to his work.

"Jacob said you were the best. That if anyone could find Nicole, you could."

He leaned over to replace the lid on the can of varnish. "I'm sure you can find someone else who'll do just fine."

"Mr. Cooper—"

"Look . . ." He swung back around. "I've got an appointment with a couple hundred square miles of sea and sky, and I'm leaving first thing in the morning. Now, if you'll excuse me, I've got work to finish."

He continued to clean up, placing cans of varnish and mineral spirits into a cardboard box and carrying them below. But when he returned topside, he wasn't surprised to find the woman still standing on the dock. She didn't look like someone who gave up easily. Anderson was going to owe him for this one.

"It's important," she said. "A matter of life and death."

"Isn't it always?"

"I don't know about *always*, Mr. Cooper. I just know about now. My sister is missing. And I need your help to find her."

"Sorry." She couldn't stand there forever, he assured himself. Meanwhile, he would ignore her. Along with his nagging conscience. "Find someone else." He'd done his time on the hero merry-go-round and knew it was a never-ending ride. He wasn't about to climb back on for some wide-eyed woman with a sexy voice.

"I'm not leaving until you hear me out," she said.

"You could wait a long time."

"Then I'll just have to wait."

"See those clouds?" He nodded toward the horizon, to the storm gathering over the Everglades. "This time of year, late-afternoon thunderstorms are a daily occurrence. In another couple of hours things are going to get a little dicey out here."

She glanced behind her and then turned back to him, her features set in a stubborn frown. "I'm not afraid of a little rain."

Cooper swore under his breath. If she had cried, he might have been able to carry through with his resolve to ignore her. He'd learned long ago how to steel himself against a woman's tears. Or if she'd pleaded, he would have cut her off without a second thought. But she just stood there, as relentless as the South Florida heat.

"All right," he said, deciding it was the only way to get rid of her. "I'll hear you out. But only so I can recommend someone else."

"But—"

"That's the deal, Ms. Burkett. Take it or leave it."

She looked ready to argue further, but then nodded. "I'll take it."

"Come aboard then." He reached up and offered his hand, but she took a step backward.

"Uh, could we talk somewhere else?"

"Somewhere else?"

She shrugged and shoved her hands into the back pockets of her jeans. "It's awfully hot, and I could use a drink." She pulled her hands free again and gestured toward the end of the dock. "I noticed a bar at the other end of the marina. I'll buy."

"Look, Ms. Burkett, I don't have time for this," he stated. "Whatever your problem is—"

"I don't like boats," she snapped. "Okay?"

He couldn't believe it. A few minutes ago she'd been like a pit bull with a bone, threatening to wait out a thunderstorm in order to talk to him. Now she was afraid to come aboard a boat—one tied to the dock, no less.

"Uh, how about that beer?" she offered again, with a forced smile. "Just one."

When he didn't respond right away, she visibly straightened and took a step toward him. "Of course, if you really want to talk here—"

"Forget it," he said, wondering if he'd lost his mind. "I think I'm out of beer, anyway." This woman wasn't going to go away just because he'd scowled at her. She was too damn stubborn. Maybe a little charm would work instead. Grabbing his shirt from one of the deck chairs, he stepped off the boat and made a sweeping gesture toward the end of the dock. "Lead on."

Jessie wasn't sure why Cooper had decided to come with her. For a few minutes, while she'd fought down her absurd fear of boats, she'd thought she'd blown it. She'd seen the exasperation on his features and expected an abrupt dismissal. Then the next thing she knew he was following her toward the small bar she'd spotted earlier. She didn't have a clue what changed his mind, but at this point she wasn't about to question her good fortune. Now they sat at a table on the outside deck of a place called Jerry's, overlooking the Intracoastal Waterway.

"Okay," he said, once a waitress in the shortest shorts Jessie had ever seen delivered two draft beers to the table. "You've got until I finish this beer. Then, as I've said—"

"I know," she interrupted, irritated despite herself that he could so easily dismiss her. "You've got an appointment with the wide-open spaces."

To her surprise, he grinned. "Yeah. I do."

It disarmed her for a moment, his smile and the laughter in his eyes. It was the first time he'd done anything but scowl at her. "You're not what I expected," she blurted out, and instantly regretted her words.

"Oh, no?" He sipped at his beer, amusement lingering in eyes almost too blue to be real. "I suppose you'd be more comfortable with a short, balding man in a trench coat."

Feeling like an idiot, Jessie nodded and took a drink of her own beer. "Something like that."

"It's too hot."

"Too hot?"

"For a trench coat."

Again he'd caught her off guard, and she couldn't help but laugh. Yes, she'd been expecting Colombo. Instead she'd found Magnum with sun-bleached hair and dancing blue eyes.

"Call me Jessie," she said.

"Okay, Jessie." He smiled, and his perfect white teeth completed the beach boy picture. "So how did you get hooked up with Jacob Anderson?"

"He's an old family friend."

"I didn't realize Anderson had any." He took another swallow of beer. "Friends, that is."

Jessie let the comment slide. She knew about Jacob's reputation as a cold fish, but he'd been like a second father to her and Nicole.

"Have you gone to the police?" Cooper asked.

The question sobered her, reminding her of why she was here. "No, but her husband has. Yesterday."

"So why come to me?"

Jessie hesitated a moment, bracing herself against the harsh reality of her sister's disappearance. "Because I'm afraid they won't find her." She needed to face both the truth and her fear. "Not alive, anyway."

Cooper stiffened and leaned back in his chair, all traces of humor gone from his features. "How long has she been missing?"

"I'm not sure. Her husband told the police a few days. But it's been three weeks since I've spoken to her."

"Wouldn't her husband know how long she's been gone?"

"If he's telling the truth."

"You think he's lying?"

"Nicole and I are very close. Three weeks is a long time for us to go without speaking to each other," she explained. "Our parents died years ago, and we have no other family. She calls me every Sunday without fail."

"So she missed a couple of weeks." He shrugged, but there was nothing nonchalant in the gesture.

"It's more than that." Jessie shifted slightly, as if to watch the passing boats on the water. In truth, it unnerved her to look at him. Despite his questions, he'd once again become the distant man she'd first encountered, and it bothered her in a way she didn't understand. "The last time I talked to Nicole, we argued. So at first I didn't think much about it when she didn't call the following week."

"And you didn't call her?"

"No, not then. Nicole always called me. She claimed she could better afford the call." Jessie shrugged. It had been only one of the many strange demands Nicole had made since her marriage. "But there were other reasons."

"Like?"

Jessie hesitated, hating to reveal her family's problems to a stranger. Yet Jacob had said Sam Cooper was the best. That if Nicole was still alive, he'd find her. Making herself look at him, she said, "Her husband and I don't get along. She calls on Sunday because he's never home on Sunday night."

He nodded, his features devoid of expression, and Jessie suddenly realized why he disturbed her. Underneath his cool facade, this man was dangerous.

Shaking the unsettling notion, she went on with her story. "The second week after Nicole and I argued, I finally called her. I figured she'd stewed long enough."

"I take it you didn't get her."

"No. So I left a message asking her to call me no matter what time she got in, but she never did. That's when I began to worry. It's not like Nicole to remain angry. For the next couple of days I tried reaching her but kept getting her housekeeper. Finally, I hopped on a plane and came down."

"You never spoke to her husband?"

"No. As I said, we don't get along."

"But if you were worried . . ."

"Believe me, it wouldn't have done any good. He wouldn't have told me anything."

This time she could see the doubt on his face, but he let it go. "Okay, so you came to see your sister in person."

"Yes, and again I spoke to the housekeeper, who gave me a story about Nicole visiting friends out of town. But the woman was obviously nervous and repeating what she'd been told to say. Plus she couldn't tell me these supposed friends' names or where they lived." Jessie shook her head, remembering her frustration with the agitated woman. "I know it doesn't seem like much, but if you knew Nicole . . . She wouldn't go anywhere without telling me. That's when I confronted Robert."

"Robert?"

"Robert Whitlock, Nicole's husband."

Cooper let out a low whistle and sank back into his chair. "You're telling me your sister is married to Robert Whitlock? *Judge* Robert Whitlock?"

"Do you know him?"

"*Of* him. Actually, I suspect most everyone in this town knows of him. He's not exactly a low-profile individual."

Jessie leaned forward. "Then you understand why I need your help?"

Cooper shook his head. "As a matter of fact, I don't know why you're even here. If anyone can mobilize the cops to find your sister, it's Whitlock."

"I don't think Robert wants the police to find her. I think he's the reason she's missing."

"Wait a minute." Cooper leaned forward in his chair. "Are you trying to tell me that Whitlock is responsible for his wife's disappearance?"

"I'm sure of it. Whether he's kidnapped her himself or she's run from him, I don't know."

"Kidnapped his own wife?"

"Okay, so maybe he's already—"

"Killed her?"

His skepticism struck her like a blow. Then anger boiled to the surface. Nothing Jessie had told Cooper had made the least little difference to him.

"Look, I'm sorry I bothered you," she said, pulling out her wallet and tossing a five dollar bill on the table. She needed help. But she'd get it somewhere else. From *someone* else.

She stood, but he grabbed her arm before she could walk away. "I'm sorry," he replied, although nothing in his expression made her believe he meant it. "Sit back down and tell me why you think Whitlock's involved." He spoke quietly, but there was no mistaking the command in his voice.

It only made Jessie angrier. "What do *you* care? You obviously don't believe me."

"Start at the beginning and don't leave anything out." Again it was an order. Something Jessie had never been very good at taking.

For several moments she glared at him, fighting the urge to walk away. She told herself she could get help elsewhere, but somewhere in the back of her mind she kept hearing Jacob's voice. "He's the best, Jessie. If Nicki's alive, Sam Cooper will find her." *Only for Nicole*, Jessie silently vowed. Yanking her arm from Cooper's grasp, she settled back in her chair.

"Nicole's been acting strange lately," she said in a low voice, refusing to look at him. If she did, she might scratch his eyes out.

"In what way?"

"It's hard to describe. It's just a feeling, really." She turned back to look at him. "Do you believe in hunches, Mr. Cooper?"

"Only my own."

She stared at him in disgust. "Why am I not surprised?"

His jaw tightened, but he kept his mouth shut.

"We argued about Robert," she said after a moment. "Several weeks earlier, she'd told me that she was worried about him, that she thought he was in some kind of trouble. But that's all she would say. The next time we talked, I asked her about it, and she acted as if I'd misunderstood. She insisted there was nothing wrong. But she was scared."

"So that's what you argued about?"

"Not exactly." Jessie glanced away before continuing. "We argued because I suggested she leave him."

"And she wouldn't."

"She hung up on me."

Cooper remained silent for a moment and then said, "That's it?"

She knew it didn't sound like much. "I know my sister. She wouldn't go anywhere without telling me. Not of her own free will, anyway."

"Let me get this straight." He leaned back in his chair and crossed his arms. "You think that Robert Whitlock, one of the most respected men in Broward County, has kidnapped or, excuse me, possibly harmed your sister in some way."

She lifted her chin and met his hard gaze straight on.

"And you believe this because she sounded strange the last few times you spoke to her on phone?"

"Scared," she corrected, holding on to her temper.

"Yeah, scared. And when you told her to leave her husband, she got angry and hung up."

Jessie leaned forward in her chair. "She *is* missing."

"And her husband has reported this to the police."

"What else could he do with me on his doorstep?"

"Any signs of abuse or mistreatment?"

"No, but—"

He shook his head, effectively cutting her off. And though her pride urged her to stand and walk away, her fear for her sister kept her firmly in her chair. She had to convince him. "Look, this may sound far-fetched—"

"You're right." He picked up his beer and finished it in one swallow. "It does."

"I know my sister," she repeated. "I raised her after our parents died." But it was like talking to a brick wall. She watched helplessly as he flagged down a passing waitress and asked for a dry cocktail napkin.

"Got a pen?" he asked Jessie.

She almost told him no, but in the end, she dug one out of her purse and handed it to him.

While writing on the small square of soft paper, he said, "Both of these men are honest and reliable." When he was done, he handed it to her.

"You're not going to help me?" She couldn't quite bring herself to believe it.

"I told you I'm on vacation." He rose from his chair. "Besides, I'm not into lost causes."

2

COOPER WALKED AWAY, the reproach in Jessie's eyes burning holes in the back of his skull. He felt like a heel. But he kept moving, despite the temptation to turn and tell her he'd changed his mind. He reminded himself that he was nobody's hero. Especially not a woman like Jessie Burkett, who cared too much to be thinking straight.

Damn! Robert Whitlock, of all people.

Not that he'd ever cared much for Whitlock. The man was too smooth for Cooper's taste. But then, so were most of the men he worked for. And she might be right. Underneath all the polish, Whitlock could be a scumbag—it wouldn't be the first time a judge turned bad. But Cooper reminded himself that it wasn't *his* job to find out. After all, he'd be taking on the whole damn system to go after Whitlock.

Nope, he didn't want anything to do with Jessie Burkett and her crazy suspicions. His specialty was finding people, not exposing crooked government officials. Of course, she would say she wanted him to find Nicole, not expose her husband. It didn't make a difference. He didn't take on private clients like Jessie Burkett. Their emotions clouded their judgment, making life hell on the investigator. And God forbid if he made a mistake or the missing person turned up dead.

But he didn't want to think about that.

If Jessie was lucky, the police would locate Nicole Whitlock unharmed. Or maybe one of the men he'd recommended would take on the case and find the missing woman. Either way, it wasn't his problem.

Back on his boat, he considered calling Anderson and giving him hell for sending Jessie his way. Instead, Cooper walked over to the recorder by his phone, with the flashing light he'd been ignoring for days, and punched the Erase button. He didn't want to talk to Anderson. Or anyone else, for that matter. What he wanted was to pull up anchor and head out toward the clear blue waters of the Caribbean.

Tomorrow, he promised himself, he'd be out of here. He'd be off to where no one could find him.

Meanwhile, he had things to do. And thinking about Jessie Burkett, with her big eyes and voice like warm honey, wasn't on his agenda.

But where women were concerned, things never did go as planned. And putting Jessie out of his mind was no exception. Just after sunset, he found himself at The Dive, a bar well off the Lauderdale strip that had long ago become a favorite watering hole for half the local cops. He told himself he'd stopped in for a beer and maybe to ask a question or two, but he knew better.

He settled onto a stool next to Hal Framen, a detective he knew on the Lauderdale force. "Hey, Hal."

The other man nodded without looking up from his drink. "Cooper. What drags you in here?"

"Can't a man stop by for a beer?"

Hal grunted and took the last sip of his drink. "Not you. You want something."

Cooper laughed lightly. "That's what makes you such a good cop, Hal. Your unfailing instincts."

"Just tell me what you want." Hal signaled the bartender for another drink and a beer for Cooper.

Once the drinks arrived, Cooper said, "I need some information."

"You working a case?"

"Nope." He took a long swallow of his beer, assuring himself it was true. "Actually, I'm on my way out of town. I'm just helping out an acquaintance before I go."

"Okay. Shoot."

"What do you know about a missing-person report filed on Nicole Whitlock?"

For the first time since Cooper had sat down, Hal turned to look at him. "How did you hear about that?"

Cooper grinned. "I have my sources."

Hal shook his head. "You wouldn't have heard about this from your normal sources. This thing's been kept real quiet."

"Why's that?"

"Judge Whitlock doesn't need the whole damn world knowing that his wife's missing. It could put her in serious danger."

"That so?" Cooper turned back to his beer, but not before noticing the slight tremor in Hal's hand. "I would think she's already in danger."

"Look, Cooper." Hal leaned closer, his voice low. "This ain't a case you need to be nosing around in."

Cooper shrugged. "Hey, I'm just looking for a little info."

"And you already know more than you should."

He turned back to look at Hal. "Finding people is my specialty, Sergeant."

"Are you sure you ain't working for someone?"

"I'm sure." Cooper finished his beer. "I'm heading out first thing in the morning."

"Good. You make sure you do that."

Cooper knew when he'd worn out his welcome. "Right. No problem." Standing, he tossed a ten-dollar bill on the bar. "The drink's on me." Then he turned and worked his way through the steadily growing crowd to the front door.

All the way back to the marina, Cooper pondered his conversation with Hal. Something wasn't right. Usually with a missing-person case, the cops would have jumped at Cooper's offer to help. Not this time. The No Trespassing sign had been as clear as the gin Hal had been downing just a little too fast.

And that was another thing.

Cooper had known Hal to put away a beer or two, maybe more, but he hardly ever drank straight liquor. And never like he'd been doing tonight.

Back on the boat, Cooper's answering machine once again greeted him with a flashing light. *Damn*, he thought, and started to walk away. Then he stopped, and cursing under his breath, turned and punched the Play button.

"Mr. Cooper," said a familiar husky voice that made him think of hot summer nights and cool satin sheets. "This is Jessie Burkett. I wouldn't bother you, but I don't know anyone else in town. I'm at the Fort Lauderdale police station and . . . I need you to come down here." She paused, and Cooper imagined her pulling herself up a little straighter. "I've been arrested."

JESSIE PACED the concrete floor, from one end of the holding cell to the other. How long had it been since she'd left the message for Cooper? An hour? Two? Out of habit, she glanced at her wrist and then shook her head. The arresting officer had taken the watch along with her other personal belongings when he'd booked her.

It had been a humiliating experience. They'd treated her like a common criminal, hustling her away from her sister's dark house in handcuffs, and then processing her with mug shots and fingerprints. She'd told them she was Nicole's sister, and they had assured her they would inform Judge Whitlock. Meanwhile, until they could verify her alleged identity—and that the judge wouldn't be pressing charges—she'd been booked for breaking and entering.

Grabbing the bars, she strained forward to see down the empty hall toward the heavy metal doors.

Instead of Cooper, she should have called Jacob—even though he was halfway across the country in Chicago. But she hadn't wanted to spend a minute longer than necessary in this place. She'd told herself that there would be plenty of time to call Jacob after she got out of here.

Of course, why she'd thought Cooper would help her escaped her reasoning at the moment. He'd looked at her today like she was nuts. And at this point, she was beginning to agree with him.

"You ain't gonna hurry things none by wearing a path in that floor," said the large woman lying on the bunk behind her.

Jessie shrugged. "I can't seem to sit still."

"Well, you're makin' me crazy."

It didn't sound like a threat. Exactly. But Jessie decided not to push it. "Sorry." Folding her arms, she moved to sit on the empty bunk.

Breaking into her sister's house had seemed like a good idea to Jessie at the time. But then, hindsight always was better than foresight. She'd just been so frustrated. No one would listen to her, and she was determined to find Nicole. So Jessie had taken the first course of action that had come to mind.

"Burkett." The sharp voice, accompanied by the rattling of keys, brought Jessie to her feet.

"Finally," she said, instantly forgiving Cooper for taking so long.

The woman officer led her through a labyrinth of corridors before opening the door to a small interrogation room. Cooper stood with his broad back to her, gazing out a dark, grainy window.

"Thank God," she said, entering the room. "I was afraid—"

"Hello, Jessie."

Startled, she spun toward the sound of the familiar male voice behind her. "Robert."

He stepped into the room and shut the door. As always, he was the picture-perfect gentleman. Tall, handsome, with just the right touch of gray at his temples, and still wearing the tux he'd worn to whatever function he'd been attending. "The police tell me you broke into my house," he said.

Jessie stood for a moment, unable to answer, a bit taken back by his unexpected appearance. She glanced at Cooper, who'd turned away from the window, but he offered no help. He met her gaze with that infuriating look of cool indifference in his eyes.

Quickly, she shifted her attention back to her brother-in-law. "I'm sorry, Robert," she said. "This has all been a terrible mistake. I tried to tell the police that, but they wouldn't listen."

He closed the distance between them and slipped an arm around her shoulders. "It must have been dreadful for you."

Jessie just managed to stop herself from pulling away. "It wasn't an experience I'd like to repeat."

"Well, the charges have been dropped." He smiled broadly, first at her and then at Cooper. "And this is?"

Cooper crossed the room and extended his hand. "Sam Cooper. It's an honor to meet you, sir."

"Cooper's a friend," Jessie added, looking up at him, daring him to call her a liar. "When I couldn't get hold of you . . ."

"I understand," Robert said, tightening his grip on her and again donning that magnanimous smile that turned her stomach. She wondered who he thought he was kidding. Certainly not her. Maybe Cooper. Or maybe the room had hidden cameras. Either way, it was a good act.

"Am I free to leave now?" she asked, moving out from under Robert's arm. "It's been quite a night, and I'm exhausted."

"Yes, I've taken care of everything except for some paperwork you'll need to fill out."

Turning to Cooper, she asked, "Would you mind taking me back to my hotel?"

Cooper cocked an eyebrow and folded his arms. "I thought you'd want to go with your brother-in-law to get your car."

She could have strangled him. The last thing she wanted was to leave here with Robert, and she figured Cooper probably knew that. So she gave him her sweetest smile and said, "I'm really tired, and Robert and Nicole's house is in the other direction. I thought it would be easier for *you* to drop me off. I'll get the car in the morning."

"In that case . . ." He dipped his head in acquiescence, and she thought she detected amusement in those insufferable blue eyes of his. Damn the man. He was toying with her.

"Well, I guess you don't need me anymore." Robert placed a hand on Jessie's shoulder and nodded toward Cooper.

"Thank you, Robert," she said, forcing the words. If he could play this game, so could she.

"No problem." He gave her shoulder a final squeeze, started toward the door and then stopped, turning back around. "By the way, Jessie, what *were* you doing at the house?"

She didn't miss a beat. She'd had plenty of time in the last few hours to come up with a viable story. "I was lonely and needed to talk to someone about Nicole." She'd decided to keep it simple. And Robert, with his loving-brother-in-law act, had played right into her hands. "So I stopped by. When you weren't home, I considered waiting in my car, but Nicole had given me a key..."

"But not the alarm code?"

"I thought I had the code. But I must have done something wrong, because before I knew what was happening, there were police everywhere."

Again he smiled, though she knew he didn't believe her. But that was all right. She didn't believe him, either. He was responsible for her sister's disappearance, and Jessie planned to prove it.

IT TOOK NEARLY forty-five minutes to get through the release process. But once all the forms were completed, Cooper escorted her out into the warm South Florida night. Jessie paused for a moment on the steps of the police station, breathing deeply of the thick, balmy air. She inhaled the fragrance of night-blooming jasmine and the tangy scent of the ocean, not more than a couple of miles to the east. Nothing had ever smelled quite so sweet.

"You coming?" Cooper asked from the step below her.

Jessie nodded and followed him across the nearly empty parking lot, where he unlocked the door of a shiny black Porsche. She climbed in, thinking the car suited him. Low and sporty, it seemed the perfect vehicle for a man with the initials *P.I.* tacked behind his name.

But the moment Cooper slid into the driver's seat, she realized her mistake. He dominated the small space, making her instantly aware of him—of his long legs and broad shoulders, of his powerful, sun-kissed arms and big hands. And of the underlying danger of the man himself.

She didn't need this, she told herself as she pressed against the door. Not now when all her thoughts should be focused on Nicole. But it was impossible to ignore him in such close quarters. He was large and alarmingly male, and the fear he instilled in her went much deeper than the simple anxiety she'd felt around Robert.

Cooper drove out of the parking lot, heading east toward the beach and her hotel. Then, without preamble, he asked, "What were you doing at your sister's house?"

Jessie didn't care for his tone of voice. Still, she kept her response civil. "You heard what I told Robert. I wanted—"

"Don't give me that," he said, cutting her off abruptly and surprising her with a show of anger. "Whitlock didn't believe a word of it. And neither do I."

"Why, Mr. Cooper." Jessie turned sideways in her seat to look at him. "I believe you just called me a liar."

"If the shoe fits."

"*Tsk, tsk.*"

"Look, after dragging me down here in the middle of the night, you owe me an explanation." He threw a quick glance at her. "Now what were you doing?"

He was right. She did owe him. He'd come to bail her out, and here she was goading him, picking an argument. Turning to stare out the side window, she said, "I was looking for clues."

"Clues?"

"I was desperate. Nicole is missing. And since no one else seems to give a damn, I guess I'm on my own."

"What about the two names I gave you?"

Jessie let out a short laugh of disgust. "You've got to be kidding."

"They're both reliable."

"No doubt." Jessie frowned, remembering her afternoon interviews. "Mr. Jennings, at least, was a perfect gentleman. He listened to everything I had to say and then politely escorted me out of his office. As for Mr. Harden, he wasn't quite so courteous."

"So you decided to break into your sister's house?"

"No one knows Nicole as well as I do. I thought if I could just look through her things, I might find a clue to her disappearance. I might see something that someone else—even her husband—might miss."

"You're crazy, you know that?" He threw another quick glance her way before turning back to the road. "What if Whitlock hadn't let you off the hook?"

"But he did."

"You were lucky."

"I can just see the headlines now, Respected Judge Has Sister-In-Law Arrested right below Respected Judge's Wife Disappears." Jessie shook her head. "I don't think so."

He considered that for a moment and then nodded. "Okay. So he probably had no choice but to let you off. Was it worth it? Did you find anything?"

Jessie sank lower in the seat. "No, I didn't have time. I wasn't in the house more than five minutes." She felt like a total idiot and figured Cooper was about to confirm it. "I don't know what happened. I thought I turned the alarm off correctly. Then I went into Robert's office, and the next thing I knew, the police were everywhere."

"Silent alarm."

"But I've heard the alarm go off before. It makes a lot of racket."

"Whitlock probably has his office separately zoned."

"I didn't even know you could do that." Jessie shook her head. She was out of her depth. "And I walked right into it."

To her surprise, he didn't say anything. She'd at least expected an I-told-you-so-smile or a shake of his head. But he let it go.

After a few minutes traffic began to pick up as they neared Los Olas Boulevard, the latest Ft. Lauderdale hot spot for the yuppie generation.

"Know anyone who drives a late-model Caddy?" Cooper asked suddenly.

Jessie shook her head. "No. Why?"

"We've got one following us."

"Following us?" Jessie turned and looked out the rear window at the crowded street behind them. "Are you sure?"

"I'm sure." Cooper glanced in the rearview mirror. "They've been with us for several miles."

"But why?"

"Maybe they just want to give us a little warning."

"A warning?"

"Yeah, like No Trespassing." He glanced in the rearview mirror again and then focused his eyes on the road ahead. "Hang on, I'm going to lose them."

3

HE'S GOOD, Cooper thought as he wove through the Saturday-night traffic, watching for an opportunity to lose the Cadillac. All he needed was a few minutes, just enough time to ditch the Porsche and pick up something less conspicuous. But the other driver kept with him, always at a discreet distance, just a few cars behind.

"I don't see anyone," Jessie said, her sexy voice filled with apprehension.

"That's the idea."

Just then a light turned yellow a few cars in front of them. "Here we go," Cooper said, as he downshifted, punched the accelerator and swung into oncoming traffic, barely avoiding a collision before speeding through the light. He took the first right and again stepped on the gas, slowing only enough to make several more seemingly random turns.

But he knew where he was headed. And he needed to get there before the Cadillac picked them up again.

"Are they still back there?" Jessie had turned in her seat to stare out the rear window.

"We've lost them for now. But keep your eyes open."

He headed west, back toward the downtown area, keeping to minor roads, his eyes scanning the dark streets for the other car. It seemed like luck was with him. But Cooper didn't believe in luck. Nor in underestimating an opponent. So once back in the more deserted downtown streets, he turned into an underground parking garage.

"We need to get rid of this car." He circled the lot down to the third level and pulled into a parking space well away from the lights. "Move it," he said, climbing out. "Before your friends find us."

"They're not my friends," she snapped, though she followed his lead and got out of the car. "Besides, I thought you said we'd lost them."

"Come on." He grabbed her arm and led her two rows over to a white Ford Taurus.

"Whose is this?" she asked, as he unlocked the passenger door and unceremoniously shoved her inside.

"Mine."

"Yours?"

He slid into the drivers seat. "Got a problem with that?"

"It's just . . . not what I would have expected."

"Exactly." He backed out of the parking space and headed for the exit. "Scoot down so no one can see you."

Jessie stared at him wide-eyed for a moment and then did as he said. Within minutes, they were back on the road, this time heading west toward I-95.

"Okay," Cooper said as he pulled onto the northbound lane of the highway. "You can get up now."

Jessie straightened and looked around. "Are they really gone this time?"

He again glanced in his rearview mirror. "Looks that way."

Evidently not trusting him, Jessie scanned the highway in all directions. Finally, she seemed satisfied and settled into her seat to stare out the side window.

After several minutes of silence she asked, "Why would someone follow us?"

If he knew the answer to that, Cooper thought, he'd be way ahead of the game. But he could make some good guesses. "As I said, it could be a warning. Someone trying to scare you into staying away from this."

"But you don't think so."

"It doesn't make sense." Shifting in his seat, he rolled one shoulder and then the other in an attempt to ease the tense muscles. "The driver was too good. He didn't plan on being spotted." Cooper smiled to himself. The guy hadn't known whom he was up against, but Cooper would bet he'd know soon enough. "Next time he'll be more careful," he said aloud. "And I won't be able to lose him as easily."

"Next time? Easy?"

He ignored her statement. "My guess is they want to find out what you know."

"But that's ridiculous. I don't *know* anything."

He glanced over at her. "Are you sure?"

"Of course I'm sure. Don't you think if I had anything concrete, I'd go to the police?"

Cooper shrugged. "Maybe they think you'll eventually lead them to her."

"That means she's alive."

He heard the hope in her voice and hated to crush it. "Not necessarily."

"But you just said—"

"I'm guessing, Jessie. There could be any number of other reasons why they were following us."

He felt her gaze on him for a few moments longer, hard and accusing. It was as if she blamed him for her sister's disappearance and for the car that had tailed them earlier. He'd been here before and didn't like it. It had been a different time and place, a different woman with a different missing loved one. But it was the same. And he knew, just as before, that if Nicole Whitlock turned up dead, Jessie would hold him responsible.

That was the main reason he hadn't wanted to become involved. The reason he needed to keep distance between this woman and himself. Yet even as he told himself as much, he suspected it was already too late.

Suddenly, she seemed to notice they weren't heading in the direction of her hotel. "Where are we going?"

"Somewhere safe."

"Are we in danger?"

"Don't know." He again glanced in his rearview mirror. "But I'm not willing to risk it. Are you?"

She slumped in her seat, and Cooper wished he'd gone a little easier on her. After all, she wasn't used to half of what she'd been through today. Hell, even he wasn't used to it. Locating missing people very seldom involved cloak-and-dagger games.

"Look," he said. "I've got a place where you'll be safe for the night. And tomorrow...well, we'll worry about that then."

"Not the boat."

Cooper laughed softly. At least she hadn't lost all of her spunk. "Don't worry, I wouldn't dream of it."

FIFTEEN MINUTES LATER he unlocked the door of an oceanfront condominium in Pompano Beach. Inside, he shut off the alarm and motioned for Jessie to enter. She stepped into the dimly lit foyer, and he closed and locked the door behind them.

"Make yourself at home," he said, nodding toward the wide-open living area.

She walked slowly into the room without turning on any more lights, while he headed straight for the wet bar. Retrieving two snifters and a bottle of brandy, he watched as she moved around the room. She ended up in front of the windows, fifteen feet of glass that, in the daylight, opened the apartment to the Atlantic

Ocean. But on a night like this, with the moon hovering somewhere behind them near the western horizon, it resembled a gigantic black hole.

She stood silhouetted against the darkness, her arms clasped tightly around her waist, looking suddenly very frail. Cooper had an unexpected urge to go to her, to wrap his own arms around her and add his strength to hers.

He squashed the thought immediately.

He'd already gotten more involved with this woman than he cared to. He wasn't about to let it go any further.

"You live here?" she asked softly, her voice a husky lure in the near darkness.

He looked away from her and concentrated on pouring the brandy. "I live on the boat."

"And this place?"

"I keep it for emergencies." He moved up behind her, holding the snifters. "Like now."

She turned then, her eyes two turbulent pools, liquid, dark and rimmed with fatigue. Again he wanted to pull her into his arms, but he doubted whether she'd allow it. She looked as if she would shatter in a million pieces at the slightest touch.

"It's quite a place," she said, "just for emergencies."

"It can't be traced back to me, Jessie. You're safe here." Again he fought the urge to comfort her with more than words and handed her one of the snifters instead. "Here, this will help."

Nodding, she took the glass and stepped away from him to settle onto the nearby couch. But she didn't relax. Leaning forward, she rested her arms on her legs while holding the snifter of brandy with both hands. "I wasn't sure you'd come for me."

"I almost didn't." He sat across from her in an armchair and sipped at the brandy.

"So, why did you?"

Cooper shrugged, uncomfortable with the question. And the answer. "Does it really matter?"

"It matters if it means you're going to help me."

He didn't have a response for her. Every instinct he possessed told him to walk out the door. Yet he was still here. And he didn't want to examine his reasons too closely. "I asked a few questions this evening," he said instead.

"And?"

"I didn't like the answers."

"You *are* going to help me."

He couldn't deny it. "Tell me more about your sister."

"I have a picture." She reached down and pulled her wallet from her purse. Flipping it open, she took out a photo and handed it to him.

He saw the resemblance immediately. And the difference. Nicole Whitlock was a beauty. Blond and green-eyed, with a come-hither smile made even more seductive by the startling innocence in her eyes, she had the kind of face that started wars, made millions or simply drove every male within range crazy.

"Beautiful, isn't she?" Jessie asked.

Surprised, he looked up at the woman sitting across from him. He had the strongest urge to lie, but somehow he knew she wouldn't believe him if he did. He had a feeling Jessie knew only too well the differences between her sister and herself.

"Yes, she's lovely."

He handed the picture back to her, and she quickly dropped it into her purse. "We had different mothers. Mine died when I was five, and father married Nicole's mother a couple of years later." She shifted her gaze to examine the glass in her hands, gently rolling it between her palms. "I was ten when Nicole was born."

Cooper hesitated. She didn't need any more questions tonight, but a woman's life was in jeopardy. And the more information he had, the better his chances were of finding her alive. "What happened to your father and stepmother, Jessie?"

"They died in a boat accident years later." Sighing, she set the snifter down on the end table and, leaning back against the couch, closed her eyes. "Nicole was nine and the authorities wanted to put her into a foster home. Jacob stopped them. He and father were friends from way back. So Jacob pulled some strings or called in favors." She shrugged. "I don't know, really, what he did. But he ended up with custody of Nicole and moved us both into his home. Up until then, we'd had a normal sibling relationship. Then suddenly, at nineteen, I became Nicole's mother."

Jessie paused for a few minutes before adding, "She's never been very strong. Someone has always looked after her, taken care of things for her. At first it was our parents. Then me. Now it's Robert." She lifted her head and looked at Cooper, tears brimming in her eyes. "If she's alive, you have to find her. She doesn't have the faintest idea how to make it on her own."

He met her gaze, and the last of his resistance slipped away. Something about her tugged at him, awakening a part of his soul he'd put to rest years ago. She needed his help, and he couldn't deny her—no matter what it did to him in the end. Only his firm grip on the arms of his chair kept him from going to her even now, from closing the small space between them and pulling her into his arms. To comfort her, he assured himself. Only to comfort her.

She was the first to turn away. Rising a little too quickly from the couch, she stumbled, and he stood to steady her. Almost instantly, she backed away, pulling her arm from his grasp.

"Is there somewhere I can get cleaned up?" she asked.

For a moment he couldn't answer, but watched as she rubbed absently at the spot where he'd touched her. Finally, he dragged his gaze back to her face. "Take the master bedroom for the night. You'll find everything you need, and there's a robe in there you can use."

She nodded and turned away, disappearing into the other room. When she was gone, Cooper retrieved his brandy and swallowed the last of it.

His touch had shaken her.

Almost as much as it had shaken him. And though he knew better than to think it meant anything, he also knew he would never convince her of that. He'd been through this before. He knew how a woman could temporarily feel something for a man who helped her. How she might even think she was in love. He called it the knight-in-shining-armor syndrome. The only problem was it never lasted. And when it was all over, he would be the one left behind.

JESSIE STARED AT the face in the mirror, hardly recognizing herself. She bore little resemblance to the woman who'd left her hotel room early this morning. Her too-wide eyes, her pale skin, the grim tension around her mouth made her look like a refugee from a war zone. And that's exactly how she felt.

She turned her back on the image and peeled off her clothes. Running the water as hot as she could possibly stand, she stepped into the shower. For several long minutes she stood with her head thrown back, letting the steaming liquid slide over her body.

What was she doing here?

She was in an ocean-side condominium with a man she'd met a little over twelve hours ago. An inherently dangerous man, she reminded herself. A man who sent shivers of heat through her with the slightest touch. A man whose mere presence made her forget her priorities. She should walk—no, run—as far and as fast as she could from Sam Cooper.

But she needed him.

He could find Nicole. And wasn't that why she'd come to him to begin with? To find her sister? Somehow she needed to keep that thought foremost in her mind. Nicole. She was here for Nicole. And whatever crazy feelings Sam Cooper aroused in her, Jessie would just have to ignore them. She could do it, too. As long as he didn't touch her again.

She stayed in the shower until the water ran cold, then towel-dried her hair and wrapped herself in a large terry-cloth robe she found in the closet. With one final glance in the mirror, she decided she looked better. And with her priorities once again straight in her head, she felt better as well.

Back in the living room, she was drawn by the smell of cooking food. Evidently, Cooper had all sorts of hidden skills. Then she walked into the kitchen, and he turned and smiled, reminding her of the beachboy she'd caught a brief glimpse of at the waterside bar earlier today. And her resolve to remain unaffected by him nearly crumbled once again.

"Just in time," he said as he scooped globs of what looked like scrambled egg onto two plates. "Have a seat."

"It smells wonderful." She hadn't even thought about food since the quick burger she'd grabbed at lunchtime. Suddenly she was very hungry.

"I figured you could use something to eat." He set a plate in front of her on the table as Jessie took in the carefully set table, the placemats, the flatware arranged just so. "It's supposed to be an omelet," he said. "But I never could get the hang of folding them. Coffee?"

"Thank you," she answered, though she barely managed to get the words past the lump in her throat.

He didn't seem to notice. "I'm afraid the food supply is rather limited. Eggs are the only perishable item I keep on hand." He retrieved the coffeepot, filled a mug and set it in front of her. "I'll stock up tomorrow."

Jessie sat, unable to touch her food as Cooper took a seat across the table from her. She couldn't remember the last time anyone had done something so nice for her, the last time someone had seen to her needs or fixed her a meal. It was the final straw in a day filled with too many burdens. The tears she'd been holding back for hours slipped out.

Before she could stop them or him, Cooper was beside her, pulling her up and into his arms. Strong, protective arms that cradled her against a chest made to hold a woman. And it only made things worse. Her sobs came faster and harder, wetting his shirt, burning her eyes and cheeks. And he just stood there, holding her, murmuring nonsensical words she couldn't hear above her own misery.

It all came out—her fear for Nicole, her embarrassment at being arrested, her total confusion over being followed, then hidden away in an unfamiliar place by a disturbing man. It all came out while she was held gently in the strongest arms she'd ever known.

And when her tears finally subsided, he lowered his head and covered her lips with his. She melted into his kiss, his soft, gentle, reassuring kiss. And she knew she was lost.

ROBERT WHITLOCK HATED to be kept waiting.

By anybody. And especially by a man who called himself "Colonel," though he had no affiliation to any military organization Robert knew of. But stupidity had never been one of his failings. So he kept his annoyance to himself as the Colonel strode into the room and sat behind his sleek, utilitarian desk.

"You haven't found her," he stated without preamble.

Robert shifted uncomfortably under the other man's scrutiny. "No, Colonel. Not yet."

"You know what this means."

"I just need a little more time." Robert scooted forward in his chair. "I have my people working on it."

"I hear her sister is in town."

"Yes, but—"

"And she's hooked up with Sam Cooper."

"Yes, but he's nothing." Robert tugged at his collar. Did the man have to keep it so damn hot in here? "A local P.I. My people can handle him."

"Don't be so sure." The Colonel leaned back, rested his elbows on the arms of his chair and propped his fingers in a steeple against his hard, flat stomach. "He's ex-FBI."

"A Fed?"

"He earned quite a reputation for himself a few years back working on a special task force. Locating missing children."

Robert cursed silently. All he needed was an ex-federal agent checking up on things.

"I can't get much information on why he left the Bureau," the Colonel continued. "It seems he has friends in high places who have sealed his file. But the word is he left because of a woman."

Robert couldn't believe it. When had things become so complicated? He was a respected judge, for God's sake. A wealthy man. And his whole world was unraveling around him. All because that stupid bitch had come nosing around looking for Nicole.

"What do you want me to do?" he asked.

"Recruit him." The Colonel smiled, a cold, deadly smile. "Cooper went private when he left the Bureau. He still locates misplaced persons. Seems he has a knack for it. But now he does it for whoever has the money to pay his rather exorbitant fees."

"But then why Jessie? She's got nothing."

The Colonel shrugged. "Maybe he, too, has a weakness for a pretty face."

Robert flushed, but before he could defend himself, the Colonel continued. "Cooper's good at what he does. Maybe the best."

"We'll take care of him," Robert blurted out.

"Don't be a fool. We'll use him. He'll find your errant wife for us."

"And if he does?"

"When he does—" the Colonel settled back in his chair once again and grinned, sending a surge of revulsion through Robert's system "—my men will take care of all three of them—your wife, her sister and Sam Cooper."

4

KISSING JESSIE BURKETT wasn't the smartest move Cooper had ever made. Yet he couldn't seem to separate his mouth from hers. The softness of her lips held him, drawing him in with a sweetness and need that stirred his protective instincts. He didn't want this, didn't need this. But she was more temptation than any man could resist.

She sighed and settled closer against him, and he knew he had to end this now or give up more of himself than he dared. He broke the kiss. But he didn't release her. Not yet. Even though having her slim body next to his was almost as tempting as her lips.

"This isn't a good idea," he said.

"I know." Her words came out in a breathy whisper, rough and smooth all at once, like the feel of work-toughened hands on silk. Then she looked up at him, her big, dark eyes telling him more than he wanted to know about how the kiss had affected her.

He took a quick, backward step away from her. From those eyes. From that voice. "Look," he said, more harshly than he'd intended. "Don't get the wrong idea."

Her eyes cleared, and she lifted her chin. "And what idea is that?"

"That this means anything." No, that didn't come out right. "I was just..." What the hell *had* he meant?

She crossed her arms and met his gaze head-on. "You were just what?"

"You were crying." *Damn.* He planted his hands on his hips and glanced around the small kitchen before turning back to her. "You looked like you needed..."

"Someone to comfort me?" She sounded calm enough, but her eyes sent their own signal. If looks could kill, he'd be missing a limb or two by now.

"Yeah." He was sinking. Fast. "You've had a rough day, and I figured you needed a shoulder to cry on."

"And someone to kiss me and make it all better?"

"Look," he said, holding up his hands defensively, "let's just forget this ever happened."

She took a step toward him. "You want to know what I think?"

He didn't. But he figured she planned to tell him, anyway.

"I think—" she moved in closer "—that you have one hell of an ego. It was nothing. A kiss. And hardly worth writing home about." With that, she spun on her heel and strode out of the kitchen.

"What about your food?" he called after her.

"You eat it. After all, you're eating for two. You and your ego." The bedroom door slammed behind her, and he heard the distinctive click of the lock sliding into place.

After a moment he walked over to the table and sank into a chair. He picked up a fork and stared at the eggs he no longer wanted. All right, so he'd made a colossal ass of himself. It hadn't been the first time and probably wouldn't be the last. At least not where a woman was concerned.

He'd known Jessie was trouble the first time he'd seen her. He should have listened to his instincts and stayed as far away from her as possible. After all, she'd been right. It was just a kiss.

Then how come he felt like he'd just stepped off a cliff without a parachute?

THE SMELL OF COFFEE woke her.

She lay there for a moment, disoriented, trying to remember where she was. Then the previous day's events returned in full force. All of it. Her flight from Chicago. Her unsuccessful attempts to hire someone to help find Nicole. Breaking into the house. Her arrest. Robert Whitlock and his infuriating smile. The black Cadillac following them through the streets of Fort Lauderdale. Sam Cooper. And his kiss.

She barely suppressed a moan, embarrassment washing her face in heat. How could she have been so stupid as to let him kiss her? She'd come here seeking help to find her sister, not to fall in lust with a sexy private investigator with an ego the size of the Caribbean. Especially when he'd made it clear that he thought of her as a love-starved old maid who'd thrown herself into the arms of the first man who offered her a little kindness. Rolling onto her stomach, she pulled the pillow over her head. She didn't know how she was going to face him this morning.

Then she tossed the pillow aside.

He really had a lot of nerve assuming that she'd fall all over him just because he'd kissed her.

Climbing out of bed, she pulled on her jeans.

So she'd let Cooper kiss her last night. What was the big deal? She hadn't been herself. She'd been exhausted and frightened for her sister. The important thing was finding Nicole. As he'd suggested, she would just forget about the kiss and keep in mind her reason for being here.

Slipping on her long-sleeved blouse, she wished she had something else to put on. Something cooler. She'd almost suffocated in these clothes yesterday. It hadn't occurred to her when she left Chicago that it would be hot here this early in the year. She'd brought one pair of shorts, but they were back at her hotel, with her suitcase.

By the time she finished dressing, she'd convinced herself that facing Cooper wouldn't be a problem. That was until she saw him.

Lounging against the kitchen counter with his hair still damp from a shower, wearing light cotton slacks and a shirt he hadn't bothered to button, he looked entirely too sexy for comfort. For a moment she forgot her earlier resolve as she remembered how good it had felt to be held against that chest.

"Morning," he said, his voice bringing her back to her senses.

Nicole, Jessie reminded herself. *Remember Nicole.* "Is there more of that?" she asked, nodding toward his coffee.

"Help yourself." He shifted sideways to reveal a full pot behind him. "Cups are in the cabinet."

He remained where he was, close, too close, watching her as she got a cup and walked over to the coffeepot. He smelled of soap and aftershave, and she had to concentrate on keeping her hands steady and her thoughts on the coffee.

"Have you been up long?" she asked, trying for casual conversation. Safe conversation.

"A couple of hours."

"Trouble sleeping?" She glanced at him and realized her mistake. He would think she was referring to the kiss. His eyes reflected his amusement. "I mean..." She hesitated, backpedaling as fast as she could.

"I'm an early riser. And I had a few calls to make."

A morning person. Great! She retreated to the small kitchen table, clutching her cup of coffee with both hands. She took her first sip and closed her eyes for a moment to fully savor it. Caffeine. There really was nothing quite like it. And she would need it to deal with this man.

"Want something to eat?" he asked. "You must be hungry."

She was, but wouldn't have admitted it to him for the world. Not after she'd refused to eat last night. "Just coffee, thanks."

He turned to refill his own cup and then joined her at the table. She took another fortifying swallow and asked, "So, where do we start looking for Nicole?"

He took his time answering her, sipping his own coffee first. Then he said, "*We* don't. I'll find your sister. You're staying here."

"Wait a minute." He couldn't be serious. "I want to come with you."

"No."

"No?" She tightened her grip on the cup and on her temper. "Just like that? No discussion? Just no?"

"That's what I said."

She pushed the cup away and knit her fingers together on top of the table. Then, with what she thought was remarkable calm, she said, "You seem to have forgotten that *you're* working for *me*."

He took another sip of coffee, holding her gaze above the rim before setting down the cup. "I don't work for you. You can't afford me, remember?"

"No, I don't remember." She deserted her chair, paced the small distance to the counter and turned, her arms folded across her middle. "And what makes you so sure I can't afford you?"

He shrugged.

It infuriated her. *He* infuriated her. "I can't just sit around here twiddling my thumbs while you go off looking for my sister."

"Look, Jessie, we do it my way or not at all."

"I can help. I know Nicole—"

"You'll be in my way."

"I know her habits, her..." She stopped midsentence, realizing that arguing with him was pointless. He wasn't listening. He'd made up his mind. Well, so had she.

"What about my car?" she asked. "It's still over near Robert and Nicole's. I need to pick it up."

"I've already taken care of it."

"What do you mean, you've taken care of it?"

"One of my associates will pick it up and move it."

"Move it?" She couldn't believe this. "Where?"

"Somewhere safe but out of the way."

Obviously, he was used to being in charge and giving orders. "What if I need it?"

"You're not going to need it because you're not going anywhere. You'll be staying here for the next couple of days."

"I'm *not* staying here." Just the idea of being stuck for another night in this apartment with him unsettled her.

Sighing, he pushed himself out of his chair, walked to the sink and dumped the last of his coffee down the drain. "Whoever followed us last night isn't playing games, Jessie. They either meant to warn us off or they think you know something." Then, turning back to face her, he added, "Either way, you could be in danger." He paused, letting his words sink in. And they did, sending a ripple of fear down her spine.

She steeled herself against it.

"The best thing for you to do," he added, "is hole up here for a while. I'll find your sister."

What he said made sense. After all, she'd come to him because Jacob Anderson had said Cooper was the best. Yet she knew herself. She'd go crazy sitting around here doing nothing.

"You win," she said finally.

He looked skeptical. "You're going to stay put?"

"That's not what I said." He may be used to giving orders, but she wasn't used to taking them. "If you won't take me with you, I'll do some investigating on my own."

"Like you did last night?"

A wave of heat touched her cheeks. Common sense told her to listen to him. Fear for her sister made her hold her ground. "I'm sorry," she said. "I can't do what you want. You go do what you have to do. I'll do what I need to do."

He met her gaze for what seemed an eternity, and it took all her willpower to keep from turning away from those steely blue eyes. Finally, he said, "Okay. I'll take you with me. But we do things my way. You'll keep your room at the hotel, but you'll stay here. You don't use your own car. You don't go anywhere on your own. And you do everything I say. Got it?"

"I need some clean clothes."

"We'll stop by your hotel and pick them up. And…" He paused, obviously to emphasize his last point. "At the first sign of trouble, you're out of it. Understand?"

Jessie nodded, though she had no intention of letting him leave her out of it. No matter what happened.

COOPER WASN'T HAPPY about having Jessie along with him. He'd feel a hell of a lot better if she were tucked safely away in the condo. But he'd seen that look on her face before and wasn't about to make the same mistake twice. On her own, she'd get herself into more trouble. At least this way he could keep an eye on her.

Of course, that was part of the problem. She was a distraction. One he couldn't afford while working a case. Especially when he had no idea what he was up against or whether they were in any real danger. Of course, with one woman already missing and another stirring things up, odds were against this being a simple day at the beach.

He pulled off I-95 and headed toward downtown Fort Lauderdale. "Before we go over to your hotel," he said, "we need to get rid of this car."

"Is this a P.I. thing? Changing cars once a day?"

He ignored the barb. "Your friends are probably watching for us. They've already made the Porsche. I wouldn't want to disappoint them."

"Will you stop calling them that?" she snapped. "They're not my friends."

Cooper grinned despite himself. He liked a woman with spunk. "I figure they'll pick us up at the hotel."

"You want them to spot us?"

"As long as they're following us, I know what they're up to."

With that, he pulled into the parking garage where they'd switched cars the previous night. Within minutes they were back in the Porsche, heading toward the airport hotel where Jessie was supposedly staying.

When they drove up to the front of the hotel, all of Cooper's senses went on alert. There was a black, late-model Cadillac parked off to one side. He figured there had to be a thousand cars just like it in South Florida. This could be any one of them. Too bad he didn't believe in coincidence.

Reaching under his jacket, he released the safety strap on his shoulder holster.

"My God," Jessie said, her eyes fixed on his left side where the gun rested beneath his jacket. "I didn't know you had that on you. Is it really necessary?"

He considered reassuring her that it wasn't, but decided he wouldn't be doing her a favor. She needed to know just how dangerous this could get. Maybe then she'd go back to the safe house and wait for him. "I'm not taking any chances." He opened the door and climbed out. "Come on."

A valet hurried toward them. "Can I park your car, sir?"

"We'll just be a few minutes." Cooper slipped the guy a twenty-dollar bill. "Watch it for me."

The valet grinned and pocketed the bill. "Yes, sir. Take your time."

Cooper draped his arm casually about Jessie's shoulders and headed for the door. "How long will it take you to pack what you need?"

"About five minutes."

"Good. I've got a funny feeling about this place." He glanced back at the Cadillac. "I want to get in and out as quickly as possible."

Jessie nodded and led him to the bank of elevators. While waiting for one to arrive, he scanned the lobby for anything or anyone that looked out of place. Everything seemed quiet. A couple of kids were working the front desk, a single bellhop manned the bell station and an older couple were reading newspapers in the lobby waiting area. Still, the spot in his gut that always warned him of trouble continued to burn.

The elevator arrived, and he followed Jessie inside. A couple of seconds later they stepped out on the eighth floor, and Cooper's uneasiness grew.

"What's your room number?" he asked.

"Eight twelve."

"Give me the key and get behind me."

She did as he asked, her hand shaking when she handed him the plastic card key. "Cooper, you're scaring me. What's going on?"

"Hopefully nothing."

As they approached the corner of the hall where they would turn toward Jessie's room, they heard the sound of a door closing, followed by hurried footsteps. Cooper stopped abruptly, motioned for Jessie to stay put and then inched forward, slipping his hand into his jacket. He looked around the corner just as two men disappeared through the stairwell exit at the end of the hall.

"Wait here," he said to Jessie, taking off down the hall toward her room. The door was locked, but he was pretty sure what he'd find on the other side. Flattening himself against the wall, he pulled out his gun and slipped the card key into the lock. Then, with one hard kick, he sent the door flying open, waited a moment and went in, gun ready.

Empty.

Except for Jessie's things. Her suitcase was lying open, facedown on the floor, its contents strewn about the room as if they'd been caught in a whirlwind. Cooper wondered if the men had found what they were looking for.

Quickly, he checked the bathroom and closet. They were empty.

"Oh, my God!"

Cooper spun around at the sound of Jessie's voice. "I told you to wait."

"I—"

"This time listen to me and stay put." He was already heading out the door. "Double lock this behind me and call the police. And don't open up for anyone until I return."

"Where—" But he was running toward the stairwell before she could complete her sentence.

He knew he couldn't catch them, but he needed to see if he'd been right about the car out front. And maybe he could catch sight of the men themselves. He pounded down the stairs two at a time, raced across the lobby and was out the front door of the hotel in a matter of minutes. Just in time to see a dark blue Camaro peel out of the driveway.

He zeroed in on the valet. "Who was in that car?"

"Don't know. Just a couple of guys." The kid shrugged. "In a hurry, though."

Cooper spun back around. The black Cadillac still sat at one end of the portico. The queasiness in his gut turned to acid. Whoever had followed them last night . . .

"Damn!" He took off, back inside before he could even complete the thought. They were still here, the men who'd followed him last night. And he'd left Jessie upstairs alone.

5

JESSIE STOOD FROZEN in the middle of the room.

She hadn't brought much from Chicago, but what she had lay strewn about in total disarray. Jeans and slacks, the pockets turned out, blouses and T-shirts, a dress, a nightgown, underwear and toiletries, all riffled through and tossed carelessly aside.

What had they been looking for?

She considered straightening up. She wanted her personal possessions put away before Cooper returned. Then she remembered that he'd told her to call the police.

Picking her way over to the phone by the bed, she lifted the receiver and dialed zero. "This is Jessica Burkett in Room 812," she said when the operator answered. "Call the police. Someone has broken into my room." She didn't wait for an answer, but returned the phone to its cradle and lowered herself to sit on the edge of the bed.

Again she looked at her things, and this time a sliver of fear slipped past the shock and slid down her spine. If whoever had done this had meant to frighten her, they'd succeeded. They'd gone through everything, pawing at her underclothes, violating her most personal possessions.

A loud knock startled her, bringing her to her feet. Automatically, she hurried toward the door, but then stopped, noticing that she'd forgotten to double lock it.

The knock came again, louder this time.

She didn't know how long she'd been sitting here, but she knew the police couldn't have possibly gotten here this quickly. She inched toward the door, reaching for the lock. "Who is it?"

"Miss Burkett?" called a gruff male voice from the hallway. "You in there?"

She threw the bolt just as the man inserted a card key and pushed hard on the door.

Jessie backed up.

"Miss Burkett?" he called again. "Open up. Hotel security."

She wanted to believe him, but had no intention of unlocking the door to find out for sure. Cooper had said not to let anyone in until he returned, and for once she planned to follow orders.

"Okay, pal," said a second male voice. "Back away from that door."

"Cooper." She breathed a sigh of relief. Thank God.

"Hey, mister," growled the stranger. "I don't know who—"

"You okay, Jessie?"

"Yes." Releasing the bolt, she opened the door.

Tension filled the hallway.

Cooper held a gun on a large, thickset man who looked like he belonged in a boxing ring rather than a hotel hallway claiming to be a security guard. But it wasn't the stranger who frightened her, it was Cooper. His facade had been stripped away, exposing the deadly dangerous man beneath. He was all coiled strength and controlled menace, and even if he hadn't had the gun the big boxer would have been no match for him, she suspected.

"Stay in the room, Jess." The command in his voice brooked no argument. "Until we figure out who this guy is."

"I got a call about a break-in. I just came up to check it out."

"You got any ID?"

The man turned sideways to reveal the plastic card clipped to his pocket. Cooper glanced at it without moving any closer. "Doesn't look like you."

"So I've gained a few pounds. Big deal."

"Seems to me," Cooper said, "it'd be real easy to put one of those things together."

"Look, just call the front desk."

Cooper nodded toward Jessie, who headed for the phone to call downstairs. A few minutes later the hotel manager arrived and verified the security guard's identity.

Only then did Cooper slip the gun back under his jacket.

"What about you?" demanded the guard. Without the weapon pointed at him, he made a stab at regaining some of his authority. "You got a license to carry that thing?"

"Feel free to check it out."

The man glowered, but the manager interrupted before anything else could be said, though he glanced nervously at the spot where Cooper's gun had disappeared beneath his jacket. "Could we step out of the hall? Please?"

Inside, both the guard and manager donned appropriate expressions of shock at the state of Jessie's room. "I do apologize, Miss Burkett," said the manager. "And I certainly hope you don't think this is a common occurrence. In fact, it's unheard of here. We pride ourselves on our excellent security."

"I'm sure you do." She couldn't blame this on the hotel. The men who'd done this wanted something from *her*, and she suspected it wouldn't have mattered where she'd been staying.

"We'll gladly reimburse you for any damages," the manager continued. "And, of course, there's no charge for the room."

"Thank you." He couldn't do anything about the real damage that had been done here, she knew. Somehow, when Cooper had told her she might be in danger, she hadn't understood what that meant. She'd heard his words, but the reality was something else again.

"Is anything missing?"

The manager's question pulled her out of her thoughts, and she shook her head. "Not that I can tell. But I didn't have anything of value with me."

"Well, that's good at least." He beamed his relief. "The police have been notified, and they should be here shortly."

Jessie nodded and took a deep breath to steady her nerves. As if sensing her mood, Cooper picked that moment to step forward and slip an arm around her shoulders. "How about giving us a few minutes alone?"

The manager took the hint and motioned to the guard. "Of course. We'll wait outside until the police arrive." With that they stepped into the hall and pulled the door partially closed behind them.

When they were gone, Cooper released her. "You sure you're okay, Jess?"

She nodded, wanting nothing more than to step back into his arms. But she wasn't about to repeat that particular mistake. Instead she moved over to one of the beds and sank onto its edge. "I just don't get it," she said. "What were they looking for?"

"Whoever did this . . ." Cooper paused until he had her full attention ". . . searched this room with a fine-tooth comb. They think you know something about Nicole."

Jessie hesitated, pulling her thoughts together, afraid to grasp the hope that Cooper offered, but unable to see another explanation. "Nicole must be alive, then."

"Looks that way." Crossing his arms, he leaned back against the dresser. "And my money says she's gone into hiding."

"But why? Because of what she told me about Robert being in some kind of trouble?"

"Could be she stumbled onto something incriminating, and things got a little hot." Cooper shrugged. "So she took off."

"Or someone kidnapped her to keep her quiet."

"It's possible. But then why are there two sets of lowlifes looking for her?"

"Two?"

"The men who trashed this room weren't the same ones who followed us last night."

"How can you be sure of that?"

"Sure?" He let out a short laugh. "None of this is for sure, Jess. I'm making educated guesses. That's what I do."

"But why wouldn't she call the police?"

"Maybe she didn't know who to trust. So she didn't trust anyone."

Jessie got up off the bed and paced to the far side of the room before turning back to face Cooper. "No. I don't believe it. If she were in trouble, she'd come to me." Jessie had always taken care of Nicole.

"Even if it meant putting you in danger?"

She had no answer to that.

"If I'm right," Cooper added, "we need to find her before anyone else does."

Jessie still couldn't imagine Nicole running off on her own. But what if she were wrong? What if her sister was out there alone, frightened, hiding for whatever reason, afraid of her own husband? They had to find her.

"Okay," she said finally. "So where do we go from here?"

"I want to talk to everyone who knew her. All her friends, her housekeeper, her hairdresser—everyone. And I want to start with Robert."

"If he'll talk to you."

"Oh, he'll talk—"

"Excuse me, Miss Burkett." The hotel manager opened the door and stuck his head in. "The police are here." He moved aside and a uniformed patrolman stepped into the room.

"Miss Burkett." The young man smiled, and Jessie wondered when they'd started recruiting high school kids for the police force. "I'm Officer Gell."

Cooper stayed out of the way as the officer asked Jessie routine questions about the break-in. Was anything missing? How long had she been in Fort Lauderdale? How long was she planning to stay? Cooper knew they'd never find the men who'd ransacked Jessie's room. And he figured even a wet-behind-the-ears rookie knew that as well.

"Cooper?"

He looked up. Hal Framen, the detective he'd talked to at The Dive last night, stood in the doorway. He was the last person Cooper would have expected to show up here. Leaving Jessie with the patrolman, Cooper moved to block Hal's view of the room. "Little off your beat, aren't you, Sergeant?"

"I was in the area and heard the call." Hal turned away from the door, leading Cooper a short way down the hall. "Thought I'd stop by and make sure Miss Burkett was okay."

"Very neighborly of you."

"Cut the crap, Cooper." Pushing back his jacket, Hal planted his hands on his hips. "I'm working the Whitlock case and Burkett's a key player. If there's some connection here, I need to know about it."

"Oh, there's a connection all right. Someone thinks Jessie knows where to find her sister."

"Yeah?"

"Can't quite figure it." Cooper thought again about the Cadillac he'd spotted in front of the hotel. He'd been sure it was the same car he'd seen last night. Maybe he'd been wrong. "They trashed the place," he said. "A little too obvious for pros." And he'd been pretty sure the man following him last night had been a professional.

"Sounds to me like a random hit."

Cooper grunted in disgust. "Right."

"Hey, a woman in town alone." Hal made a sweeping gesture with one hand. "Someone sees her and decides to toss her hotel room looking for jewelry or cash." Shrugging, he slipped his hands into his pocket. "Happens all the time."

Cooper eyed the other man, wondering where he'd stashed his brains for the day. "And it's just a coincidence that it happens to be Nicole Whitlock's sister."

Again, Hal shrugged. "Why not?"

"You don't believe that any more than I do."

"I'm just calling it like I see it."

"Then maybe you need to open your eyes." Cooper pushed away from the wall and started toward the door.

"So what are you doing here, Cooper?"

Hal's question stopped him, and Cooper turned back around. "I'm a friend of the family."

"Yeah. Sure." Hal lifted an eyebrow and glanced back through the door toward Jessie. "Nice-looking woman."

Cooper held his tongue. He didn't like what the detective was implying. But then, he'd never had much use for Hal Framen.

"Doesn't hold a candle to her sister, though," Hal continued. "That Nicole's a real looker."

"What's your point, Framen?"

"No point. Just an observation."

"Well, maybe you should keep your observations to yourself." Again Cooper started toward the door.

"I thought you were on your way out of town."

He stopped, but didn't give Hal the courtesy of turning around. "Plans change."

"Well, you're wasting your time on this one." Once more the police detective nodded toward Jessie. "And that little lady in there's wasting her money."

Cooper turned back to face the other man, who was definitely starting to get to his nerves. "Why's that?"

"Rumor on the street is that Mrs. Whitlock took a walk."

"That so?"

"Can you blame her? Young woman like that, married to a man twice her age? Even though he's rich. Made *me* start to wonder. So I started checking. Seems the lady liked to play around."

Cooper glanced through the door at Jessie.

"My sources say Nicole found herself a young stud," Hal said. "Get my drift?"

"I get your drift, Framen." Cooper crossed his arms. "But I'm not buying it." There were just too many people interested in Nicole Whitlock's whereabouts.

"Well, that's your prerogative. But then, if it were true, you'd be out a fat fee. Wouldn't you?"

Cooper held on to his temper. "Are you done, Sergeant?"

"Not quite. Since your lady friend's missing sister is married to the eminent Judge Whitlock, I need to verify a few facts." Framen nodded toward Jessie's room. "She just might have some information about what her sister's been up to lately."

"She doesn't know anything."

"Don't know till we ask." He started to move forward, but Cooper grabbed his arm.

Hal stopped, glanced down at where the P.I. gripped him and then pulled his arm free. "Obstructing justice, Cooper? Always thought your straightarrow reputation was a little overblown."

"I'll bring her downtown," Cooper said. "Tomorrow."

"I'd like to talk to her now."

"No." The last thing Jessie needed right now was to hear Hal Framen's theory on why Nicole had taken off. Besides, if there was any truth to Hal's allegations, Cooper wanted to hear it from Jessie first. "She's been upset enough today."

Hal met his gaze. For a moment neither man gave an inch. Then Framen backed up, suddenly changing his mind. "Okay. Have it your way. Tomorrow morning. Nine sharp."

Cooper nodded. "She'll be there."

But as he watched Framen walk away, Cooper wondered why a police detective looking for the wife of a powerful judge would allow someone to block the interrogation of a potential witness. And in particular, why would the bullheaded Framen allow it? It was out of character. Just as it had been out of character for him to throw down straight shots of gin.

IT SEEMED TO JESSIE that it took forever to finish with the police and get checked out of the hotel. Cooper had been unusually quiet through the whole process—ever since she'd seen him speaking to that man in the hall. Whatever they'd talked about had left Cooper pensive and uncommunicative.

She planned to ask him about it as soon as they were alone, but when they walked outside, Cooper stopped, obviously looking around for something. Then he crossed over to the valet, and Jessie followed, wondering what was going on.

Pulling out a wad of bills, Cooper stuffed one into the kid's shirt pocket. "When I drove up, there was a black Caddy parked over there." He nodded toward the end of the portico.

"Yeah." The kid shrugged. "They left awhile ago."

"They? What did they look like?"

"I don't know, man." The kid's gaze dropped to the roll of money still in Cooper's hand. "Just a couple of guys. You know, in suits."

"Suits?" Cooper peeled off two more bills and added them to the first. "Businessmen?"

"No way." The kid smiled. "They were too big. And you know, rough."

"Latin?"

He shook his head. "Nah."

"Are you sure?"

"Hey, man, I've lived down here all my life. I know Cubans when I see 'em. Those guys were pure New York."

"Thanks. Let's go." Cooper turned and, taking Jessie's arm, led her toward the Porsche.

Jessie waited until they were out of earshot of the valet before asking, "Do you always do that?"

Cooper glanced down at her. "Do what?"

"Bribe people."

He let out a short laugh, opened the car door and held it for her as she climbed in. "As they say, money talks." Closing the door, he circled around and climbed in the driver's side.

"So what *was* all that about the car and the men in suits?"

He took his time, starting the Porsche and pulling away from the hotel before answering. "I spotted that car—the black Cadillac—when we first drove up." He checked the rearview mirror. "I had a hunch it was the same one that tailed us last night."

Jessie couldn't help it; she turned to look out the back window. There were cars all around them. How could he tell if one in particular was following them? Twisting back around, she asked, "Were they the men who broke into my room?"

"Nope. Whoever tailed us last night was a pro. If he'd broken into your room, we never would have known about it."

Then Jessie remembered the other question she'd meant to ask. "What about the man you were talking to in the hotel? Who was he?"

Cooper threw her a quick glance. "Hal Framen. The detective assigned to find your sister."

"What did he want?"

"To talk to you."

"Me?"

Again he glanced at her. "He thinks you might know something that would help find Nicole."

"Great!" Jessie crossed her arms and settled further into the soft leather. "Now the police think I know something, too."

"I convinced him to let me bring you downtown tomorrow morning." He hesitated a moment and then asked, "How did Nicole feel about her husband?"

Something told Jessie she wasn't going to like this. She turned sideways to look at him. "What do you mean?"

Again he hesitated. "Did she love him?"

"That's an odd question."

"The woman has disappeared. All questions are fair game."

She nodded, reminding herself that the important thing was finding Nicole. "Okay, then. Yes. In her own way, Nicole loved Robert. He took care of her."

"Did she ever mention other men?"

Jessie had been right. She didn't like the direction this conversation was taking, and she couldn't help the irritation in her voice. "What exactly are you getting at, Cooper?"

"Did Nicole cheat on her husband?"

"No! Never. What gave you that idea?"

Cooper shrugged but kept his eyes on the road. "She's young, attractive and twenty-five years younger than Robert."

"Of all the . . ." Frustrated, Jessie turned away from him. So now Nicole was going to be accused of infidelity. "You don't know Nicole," she said, determined to defend her sister. "Robert's age was one of *my* objections to their marriage. But for Nicole, it was a plus."

"How so?"

"I told you. She needs someone to take care of her."

"She might have met someone else."

"No." Jessie shook her head. "She wouldn't."

"Someone younger."

"Nicole is loyal to a fault. Besides, she would have told me if there had been someone else."

Cooper didn't say anything more for a moment, and she thought he'd decided to let it rest. She'd been wrong. "How long has Nicole been married to Whitlock?"

Jessie took a deep, steadying breath. "Three years."

"And they've lived here the whole time?"

"I don't see—"

"Answer the question, Jessie." There was a trace of anger in his voice. "Yes or no."

"Yes, but—"

"When was the last time you saw her?"

"About a year ago."

For a moment he didn't say anything, as if carefully evaluating his next words. "Maybe you don't know your sister as well as you think."

"That's ridiculous. I practically raised Nicole."

"You were like a mother to her."

"Yes."

"And do women tell their mothers everything?"

His words stopped Jessie cold. Nicole would tell her, wouldn't she? If she were in trouble? If there was a man other than her husband? Jessie remembered the last time she'd spoken to her sister. There had been angry words exchanged. And tears. Could Cooper be right? Could she be that wrong—that naive—about her sister?

The sharp ring of a cellular phone snapped her out of her thoughts. She hadn't even noticed the phone until then.

Cooper picked it up. "Yeah, Alice," he said into the receiver.

She watched his face, looking for some indication of what was being said on the other end of the line. "Okay," he agreed, after a few minutes. "Call him and let him know I'll be there—" he glanced at his watch "—in about an hour. Oh, and Alice, is Victoria in?" There was a moment's pause. "She got anything going on this afternoon . . . ? Good. Tell her I'm collecting on that favor she owes me." He laughed lightly. "Yeah, pick one. Tell her I'm bringing in a client she needs to take to lunch and baby-sit for a while."

"Baby-sit?"

"Yeah, okay," he said into the phone. "Be there in ten."

Cooper hung up the phone, swung the car around and headed back downtown. "I'm afraid I'm not going to be able to take you to lunch, after all."

"Baby-sit?" Jessie repeated.

"Yeah. It seems I get my wish. Robert Whitlock wants to see me."

6

Jessie spun around in her seat. "Robert wants to see you?"

"Interesting, isn't it?"

More than interesting, it was unnerving. "But why?"

"Don't know." Cooper glanced at her, and she saw the thoughtful determination in his eyes. "But I plan to find out."

She didn't want him talking to Robert without her. "Take me with you."

"No."

"Please, I—"

"For once will you listen to reason?" There was an edge of anger in Cooper's voice that cut her off cold. "You are probably one of Whitlock's least favorite people right now. He's *not* going to talk to me with you around." He emphasized his point with another glance her way, this one hard and unyielding. "Think of your sister. And let me do my job."

Jessie turned away, unable to look into those steely eyes of his a moment longer. He was right, but that didn't make it any easier to back down. Or to allow him to go off and talk to Robert alone.

"Okay," she said finally. Because it made sense. Because she had no other choice. "Drop me off somewhere. Preferably near a restaurant. And I'll wait for you."

"I've got a better idea."

With that, he turned the car into an underground parking lot. It was the same one where they'd changed cars last night and earlier today. She decided not to ask.

"I keep an office upstairs," he said, as if reading her thoughts.

"You have an office?"

Cooper pulled the car into a parking space. "Every P.I. needs a place to hang his trench coat."

"Very funny. Seriously, if you have an office, why couldn't I find it? Why did I have to hunt you down on your boat yesterday?"

He turned toward her then, meeting her gaze with eyes the color of a turbulent sea and just as dangerous. "I guess there are a great many things you don't know about me, Jess."

Any response she could have made lodged in her throat. Suddenly, the car was too small, the space around her devoid of air and filled instead with this man. His broad shoulders and sun-bronzed skin. His hands, large and work roughened, deceptively innocent in their stillness. The intensity of his eyes, staring at her as if he could see into her soul. And the overwhelming sense of danger surrounding him.

He frightened her.

No. That wasn't true. Her reaction to him was what frightened her. Because within her, something old and primal tightened, thrilling at the prospect of his closeness, responding to the threat that was Sam Cooper. And she knew she had no defense against it.

"Come on." The edge was still there, in his eyes, in his voice. A command meant to be followed. "I'll take you upstairs." He climbed out of the car and walked around to open her door.

"I share an office with another private investigator," he said as they crossed the garage to the elevators. "She'll feed you and keep an eye on you while I talk to your brother-in-law."

Jessie finally found her voice. "A baby-sitter?"

"If that's how you want to think of it."

With that the elevator doors whooshed open, and he took her arm and led her inside. A few minutes later he escorted her through impressive double doors made of some dark and expensive-looking wood.

"Your name's not on the door," Jessie said as he ushered her inside.

"I like my privacy."

"Silly me. How could I forget?"

"Hey, Alice," he said to the pretty brunette behind the reception desk. "We made it in eight minutes."

"I think it was closer to seven and a half," she said with a smile that included Jessie. "But you always were a fast mover."

He rested a hip against her desk. "Don't go telling stories on me. You'll give my client here the wrong idea."

"Sorry." But she didn't look the least repentant.

"This is Jessie Burkett," he said. "She doesn't believe I actually have an office."

"Believe it," Alice said, turning to Jessie. "He's never in it, but we keep it dusted just in case he decides to grace us with his presence."

Jessie smiled slightly, still too disturbed by her exchange with Cooper to do more. But he'd already changed roles, like she'd seen him do before. At Alice's teasing, he'd donned a pained expression, his easygoing persona firmly in place. It wasn't genuine, Jessie reminded herself. It was an act. She'd seen the real man this afternoon. Twice. A menacing man, holding a gun on an oversize security guard. And a perilously tempting man, with eyes a woman could drown in.

"Is Vicki expecting us?" he asked Alice.

"She's waiting in her office."

"Good." Taking Jessie's arm again, he started across the reception area toward a closed door.

"Cooper," the receptionist said behind them. "Tread lightly. She's on the warpath."

"Another divorce case?"

"You got it."

Cooper rolled his eyes and continued toward the door.

As they entered the large, modern office, a tall, imposing woman stood and came around the desk. "I thought you were on your way to the islands," she said without preamble.

"Hello to you, too, Vicki."

She ignored his rebuke and planted her hands on her hips. Obviously, Cooper didn't intimidate her one little bit. "So, what are you doing here?"

Motioning toward Jessie, he said, "Vicki, meet Jessie Burkett. Jessie, this is Victoria Fernandez. Despite her lack of manners, she's the second-best detective in South Florida."

"Hah!" Victoria turned and extended her hand to Jessie. "Don't believe him, Jessie. His overinflated male ego often gets in his way. Ask anyone."

"No need." She shot a glance at Cooper. "I've noticed."

"Ladies," Cooper interjected, "if you can stop maligning my character for a moment, I've got work to do. Jessie is Nicole Whitlock's sister." Then, as if he needed to clarify, he added, "As in Judge Whitlock's missing wife."

That seemed to spark Victoria's interest. "Oh, really? So the islands are on hold?"

"The islands are on hold."

"Okay," she said, suddenly all-business. "Sounds more interesting than the divorce case I'm working. What would you like me to do?"

"I need to go talk to Whitlock. And since he and Jessie here aren't on the best of terms, I'd hoped you'd watch her for a few hours for me."

"This isn't necessary," Jessie said. "I'll be fine on my own."

Ignoring her, Cooper continued talking to Victoria. "It looks like the judge's wife has gone into hiding. And there are several interested parties who seem to think Jessie can enlighten them as to her whereabouts."

Victoria turned to Jessie and smiled warmly. "There's a private dining room upstairs. We'll go eat and then come back here. If that's okay with you?"

"Really," Jessie insisted, "you don't have to do this."

Evidently, neither Victoria nor Cooper cared what she thought. "Thanks, Vicki," he said before shifting his attention back to Jessie. "You'll be safe here. Victoria's the best."

"Next to you, of course." Jessie let the sarcasm drip from her voice.

"That goes without saying." He smiled his I-want-you-to-believe-I'm-just-a-regular-guy smile and headed for the door, where he paused. "And Vicki?" He turned back to face them. "Watch her." He nodded toward Jessie. "She has a tendency to get into trouble when left to her own devices."

Before Jessie could respond, he was out the door.

"Does he always do that?" Jessie asked.

"You mean take off without giving anyone else a chance to comment, give an opinion or get a word in edgewise?"

"Yeah," Jessie said.

Victoria nodded. "Always."

"Great."

Victoria studied her for a moment and then asked, "Hungry?"

"Starving." In fact she couldn't remember the last time she'd eaten. Sometime yesterday.

"Come on. Let's head upstairs, and you can tell me all about your sister and the good judge."

"Only if you promise to tell me all about your partner."

Victoria grinned. "We ain't partners, honey. Cooper doesn't take partners. But I can tell you a thing or two."

COOPER HAD NEVER QUITE gotten used to the ostentatious displays of the wealthy. Although he should have. In the five years since he'd left the Bureau and gone to work in the private sector, he'd been surrounded by the very rich and their trappings. Still, it made him uncomfortable. Ironically, with the money he'd stashed away over the last few years he'd probably be classified as well-off himself.

The honorable Judge Robert Whitlock, however, was much more than well-off. His family had been wintering in South Florida since the nineteen twenties, and at some point they'd settled in to stay. Since then, three generations of Whitlocks had dabbled in politics in Fort Lauderdale—a playground for the very rich.

So Cooper shouldn't have been surprised by the house.

Just south of the Broward County line, in one of the few stretches of oceanfront property that could claim private residences, the Whitlock home spoke of old money. The land itself was worth millions. Add to that a ten-, maybe twelve-thousand-square-foot mansion, and Cooper couldn't even imagine the kind of money it took to own the place. Nor did he want to. Unlike many of the homeowners in the area, Whitlock had restored the original structure. It was old-world Florida with acres of tiled roof, sweeping verandas and pale peach stucco.

A housekeeper answered the door. She'd evidently been expecting him. After inspecting his identification, she led him down marble-floored halls to what he assumed was Whitlock's office.

She knocked lightly and then opened the door. "Señor Whitlock, Mr. Cooper is here."

"Thank you, Rosa." Whitlock stood and came around his desk, his hand extended. "Mr. Cooper, it's good to see you again."

"Judge Whitlock."

"Please, don't be so formal. Robert will do."

Cooper nodded. "Robert."

"Please," Whitlock continued, motioning toward a chair. "Sit down."

Again Cooper complied, and Whitlock returned to his seat. "I'm sure you're wondering why I asked you here."

"The thought had crossed my mind."

Whitlock folded his hands carefully in front of him, studying them for a moment before answering. "Well, I imagine Jessie has told you about Nicole."

"She's told me that her sister is missing, yes."

Whitlock sighed audibly. "I'm beside myself with worry."

"That's understandable."

"I'm afraid this might involve someone who has a grudge against me. Possibly someone I sent to prison."

"That's always a possibility." Although Cooper didn't buy it. "Have you received a ransom call or note?"

Whitlock shook his head. "No. Nothing."

"Seems like you would have . . ." Cooper watched carefully for Whitlock's reaction ". . . *if* someone had kidnapped her."

"Unless . . ." Whitlock closed his eyes for a moment and then reopened them. His pain caught Cooper unaware. "Unless they've already killed her."

Cooper had to grant it to him—if this was an act, Whitlock was one hell of an actor. "I think you can rule that out," he said, surprised at his own impulse to offer Whitlock reassurance. "If one of your enemies had killed Nicole, you would have received a note of some kind. After all, what good is revenge if it's kept a secret?"

Whitlock nodded and smiled tightly, his self-control once again firmly in place. "Of course. You're right."

"However," Cooper said, "I doubt you needed me to tell you that. So why am I here?"

Whitlock hesitated a moment or two longer and then said, "I did some checking around after we met last night. Watching out for Jessie. You understand."

Cooper didn't believe it for a minute. "Of course."

"You've made quite a reputation for yourself."

Cooper nodded, dismissing the compliment. "I do my best."

"Don't we all. . . ." Whitlock seemed distracted for a moment, then smiled self-consciously and refocused on Cooper. "The reason I asked you to come here is that I want to hire you to find my wife."

Cooper sat a little straighter. He hadn't expected this. A man like Whitlock could have every law-enforcement agency in the county jumping through hoops. Besides, he'd seen Cooper with Jessie last night.

Before he could respond, however, Whitlock continued. "I'm going to be perfectly honest with you, Mr. Cooper."

"Please do."

"We both know that the police are...overworked?" He met Cooper's gaze and held it. "I want my wife back, and I'm told you are the man who can find her for me."

"Well, I appreciate the vote of confidence," Cooper said. "But I already have a client."

"Jessie?"

"Yes, sir."

"I see." Whitlock frowned, again studying his folded hands. "I didn't want to mention this, but it seems I have no choice." He looked up then and pinned Cooper with his gaze. "My sister-in-law is unbalanced."

Cooper shifted in his chair but didn't respond. He'd come to listen to Robert Whitlock's side of things, and no matter how disturbing, he intended to hear it.

"Actually," Whitlock said, "I blame myself."

Again Cooper remained silent.

"Did Jessie tell you how Nicole and I met?" Then, without giving Cooper a chance to reply, he added, "Of course she didn't. And who could blame her?" Whitlock sighed and ran a hand through his hair. "You see, Mr. Cooper, Jessie introduced me to Nicole. And, well..." He glanced away, obviously hesitating. "I guess there's no easy way to say this. Jessie and I were engaged to be married at the time."

Years of discipline kept Cooper from reacting. On the outside, anyway. Inside, he felt like someone had kicked him in the gut. Then he had to clamp down on an unexpected surge of anger. He didn't like being lied to, or working with only half the facts. And he didn't like women like Jessie Burkett, who kept important details from him.

"I'm not proud of what happened," Whitlock said. "But Jessie and I—" he lifted his hands in a gesture of helplessness "—well, how can I say this? I cared for Jessie, but I never loved her. And I doubt she ever truly loved me."

"Yet you were going to marry her," Cooper said, forcing the words past the knot of anger in his chest.

"My first wife died very young. I was devastated and never expected to love another woman." He carefully refolded his hands. "I met Jessie several years later, through mutual friends. I get up to Chicago fairly regularly, and we knew each other for years before deciding to marry. We were comfortable with each other. I never expected more." He paused. "Then I met Nicole."

"And you fell in love?" Cooper couldn't keep the skepticism out of his voice.

"Yes," Whitlock answered, looking up to meet Cooper's gaze. "I know how this sounds. A man my age falling head-over-heels in love with a beautiful young woman. A woman young enough to be my daughter." He let out a short, self-deprecating laugh and glanced away. "As they say, there's no fool like an old fool."

Cooper remained silent. There wasn't anything he could say that Whitlock didn't already know himself.

"Nicole is so beautiful," Whitlock said, and then looked back at Cooper with a new intensity in his eyes. "But it's more than her beauty. There's an innocence and purity about her that makes her very special."

He fell silent. Cooper gave him a few minutes, still struggling with his own sense of betrayal. Finally, he said, "That doesn't make Jessie unbalanced."

Whitlock leaned back in his chair. "When I called off our engagement and told Jessie how I felt about Nicole, she didn't take it well."

"Do you blame her?"

"No." The judge shook his head. "Not at first. I'd never meant to, but I'd hurt her badly. I understood that. So Nicole and I decided to wait a year before going forward with our marriage plans. But Jessie never came around." He leaned forward again, to rest his arms on his desk. "In fact, she did everything in her power to stop our marriage. She failed, but she still couldn't accept it. So instead of wishing us the best, she has spent the last three years badgering and begging Nicole to leave me. She's made our lives miserable, making Nicole doubt herself and me." His voice had grown angrier with each word. Now he paused, obviously making an attempt to calm himself. Finally, with a sigh, he settled back in his chair. "Have you ever been married, Mr. Cooper?"

"No."

"Marriage is not easy. Jessie has made ours almost impossible. Nicole adores her sister and would do anything for her. Jessie has used that fact. And it has nearly torn Nicole apart." He paused again, as if giving Cooper time to assimilate his words. "It's taken years for Nicole to stand up to Jessie." His eyes narrowed. "And *this* is the woman you're working for."

Having made his argument, Whitlock fell silent once more.

Cooper hesitated, picking his words carefully. "I'm sorry, Judge Whitlock. But none of this has any bearing on my professional relationship with Miss Burkett. Or on whether I can find your wife."

At first Whitlock looked stunned. Then his anger returned. Despite the judge's attempt to hide it, Cooper saw it in the hard glint of his eyes and the throbbing pulse in his temple.

"Jessie can't afford you," Whitlock said. "Work for me . . ." he paused, making sure he had Cooper's full attention ". . . and you can name your price."

Cooper didn't move, gauging his own response, tightening his control. He didn't like what Whitlock was implying. The fact of the matter was he didn't like Whitlock, period. He didn't want the man's money, and he wasn't about to be bought.

But it wouldn't do him any good to let the honorable judge in on his thoughts. So Cooper smiled, or gave what he hoped was a close facsimile of a smile. "It doesn't really matter who I'm working for, now does it?" Of course, both of them knew differently. "As long as I find your wife."

Whitlock glared at him, evidently unfamiliar with rejection of any kind. Finally, he smiled tightly, once again playing the game. "Of course, that *is* what's important." Then, after a moment's pause, which Cooper suspected he needed to draw his emotions more tightly under control, he said, "If there's anything I can do to help you, all you need do is ask."

"In fact there is." Cooper broadened his smile, acting as if he hadn't just stepped on the toes of one of the most powerful men in Broward County. "I need to talk to the people who knew your wife—friends, neighbors, staff, even her hairdresser. I was hoping you could supply those names."

"Rosa will help you." Whitlock picked up the telephone on his desk and pressed a button. After a moment, he spoke into the receiver. "Send Rosa in, please."

They sat in tense silence until the housekeeper appeared in the doorway. "You asked to see me, *señor?*"

Whitlock stood, and Cooper followed suit. "Rosa, Mr. Cooper is helping the police look for Mrs. Whitlock. He needs information. Please cooperate with him any way you can."

"Of course."

Whitlock shifted his attention back to Cooper. "I don't suppose you'll change your mind?"

"No, I don't suppose I will."

Anger flashed again in Whitlock's eyes, and Cooper wondered if he would end up regretting this particular decision. Then he pushed the thought aside. He'd made wrong decisions before and paid the price. But this one felt right.

"Thank you for coming," the judge said. Without moving from behind the desk, he extended his hand, forcing Cooper to step forward. "And I expect everything we've talked about here to be kept strictly confidential."

"Of course." With that, Cooper turned and followed the housekeeper out of the office.

As Rosa led him back the way they'd come earlier, he shoved all thoughts of Jessie aside. He would deal with her later. Right now he wanted to know who Nicole Whitlock associated with. He told Rosa the type of information he needed. When they reached the front hall, she said, "Señora Whitlock kept her address and appointment books in her study. If you wait here, I will get them for you."

She started to turn, but Cooper stopped her. "I'd like to come with you, if I may."

She lifted her eyebrows in surprise. "Upstairs?"

Cooper smiled and slipped his hand into his pockets. "Sometimes it helps to see the missing person's room." He shrugged. "I might find a clue as to what happened."

She hesitated, clearly uncomfortable with the idea of this stranger in Señora Whitlock's suite.

"If it will make you feel better," he offered, "let's go ask Judge Whitlock."

She thought about that for a moment and then shook her head. "No. He is a very busy man." Turning, she headed toward the stairs. "This way, please."

Nicole's sitting room surprised him.

Everything about the house so far had whispered of old money. Then Rosa had led him into a room that hinted of something else, only Cooper decided he would need an advanced degree in psychology to figure out exactly what. The room was as elegant as the rest of the house except for one thing: stuffed animals. Dozens of them, all shapes and sizes, filling every nook and cranny.

He'd never seen anything quite like it.

"*Señora* collects them," Rosa said, as if reading his thoughts.

"Evidently." He didn't know what else to say.

Ignoring his comment, Rosa walked over to the desk by the window. Opening the drawer, she pulled out two small books and offered them to Cooper. "Will these do?"

Accepting the books, he took a few minutes to glance through them for the information he needed. Another surprise. Nicole Whitlock had been both efficient and meticulous. In a small, feminine hand, she'd recorded names and addresses of everyone from Jacob Anderson to the grocery-delivery boy.

It was odd.

He'd expected names and addresses of other socially prominent people. Or old friends. Jacob Anderson would certainly qualify. But why would Nicole Whitlock keep, in her personal address book, information of every service person she or her household used?

"Did you show these to the police?" he asked, looking up from the books.

Rosa straightened and met his gaze. "They didn't ask."

Cooper shook his head in disgust. "Can I borrow them?" Before she could object, he added, "I'll have them copied and returned tomorrow."

Again she hesitated, and Cooper tried to curb his impatience. "Please, go ask Judge Whitlock."

"No," she said abruptly. "Just return them."

"Thank you." He nodded, and she started toward the door. "One more thing, Rosa."

She stopped and turned. The lack of expression on her face told him she was eager to be rid of him. "I need to speak to the staff."

"There is only the cook, one house girl and myself."

He crossed the room to stand near her. "That'll be fine."

She pursed her lips and then nodded. "Of course."

As she led him back down the hall, Cooper heard the sound of hushed, but angry voices filtering up the staircase. He glanced at Rosa, who pretended not to hear. Then they came to the top of the stairs, and the voices quieted.

Robert Whitlock stood below them in the front hallway, his back to the staircase. He was facing another man whose face Cooper couldn't see. But just then, as if sensing his and Rosa's presence, the second man looked up and met Cooper's gaze.

Hal Framen.

7

THE RESTAURANT WHERE Victoria took Jessie occupied the entire top floor of the building. It featured a panoramic view of downtown Fort Lauderdale, with the Atlantic Ocean as a backdrop. Under different circumstances Jessie would have enjoyed lingering all day, sitting next to the floor-to-ceiling windows, drinking in the sunshine and sharp, clear blue of the sea and sky.

Unfortunately, she barely noticed the scenery. Instead she spent the whole hour and a half trying not to think about Cooper.

She failed miserably.

Pushing her empty plate out of the way, Jessie leaned forward to rest her arms on the table. "Tell me about Sam Cooper," she said to Victoria.

"Pay-back time?"

Jessie smiled. "Something like that."

During lunch, Victoria had asked dozens of questions about Robert and Nicole. Jessie hadn't really minded. Victoria had listened to everything Jessie said, without appearing to pass judgment. But it continually brought Jessie's thoughts back to the discussion that must now be taking place between Robert and Cooper.

"What would you like to know?"

"I don't care." Jessie shrugged. "Anything you want to tell me." Right now she just needed to talk about something other than her sister and Robert Whitlock. And Cooper seemed like a good topic. "How long have you known him?"

Victoria settled back in her chair and crossed her long legs. "Nearly ten years. We met while he was still with the Bureau."

"Bureau?"

"The FBI. Didn't you know?"

"No. He never mentioned it."

"I shouldn't be surprised." Victoria smiled knowingly. "He rarely talks about it. My guess is that he wants to put that part of his life behind him."

"Why?"

Victoria shook her head. "You'd have to ask him. He's never volunteered the information. And I've never asked."

Jessie had known Cooper for less than twenty-four hours, but his reticence to speak about himself fit what little she knew of him. A man was riddled with contradictions. And as he'd said, there were a great many things she didn't know about him. Maybe that was for the best. After all, everyone had their secrets. She should leave his alone.

But for reasons she refused to examine, she couldn't.

"How long did he work for the FBI?" she asked.

"They recruited him right out of college. I met him five, maybe six years later. We worked on a case together." Victoria grinned and added, "From different sides of the street."

"Tell me about it."

"Well . . ." Victoria paused, whether to gather her thoughts or decide how much to say, Jessie couldn't tell. "In some ways it was a pretty standard case. A seven-year-old girl named Maria had disappeared from a playground in Little Havana." Again she hesitated, this time her eyes darkening at the obviously unpleasant memory. "Children disappear too often. This time, however, Maria was the second child to vanish from the same family within a year. The local authorities suspected the mother of foul play."

Jessie shuddered at the thought.

Evidently Victoria noticed. "Yeah, it's a horrible thought, that a mother could harm her child. Her *children.* In this case, I didn't believe it. I knew the family."

"You knew them?"

"Not well, but I grew up in Little Havana. It's a small community. Anyway, it was a very tricky situation—" leaning forward, Victoria crossed her arms on the tabletop "—and my first big case. Maria's grandparents had hired me. Partially because they couldn't afford anyone with more experience, and partially because I was from the neighborhood."

"And Cooper?" Jessie asked.

"The Bureau had created a special task force to locate missing children, and he was their star investigator. They'd been drawn into the case because there had been some evidence indicating that Maria had been transported out of Florida."

Victoria paused for a moment to stare out at the sun-drenched city, then she turned back to Jessie. "At first, when the FBI found out the family had hired a private investigator, there was friction. They don't like outsiders treading on what they consider their turf." She shook her head and laughed abruptly. "Fortunately, Cooper's only concern was for the girl, so we ended up working together."

Jessie was almost afraid to ask the next question. "Did you find her?"

"Cooper found her. Actually, he found both her and her older sister."

"Were they—"

"Alive?" Victoria nodded. "Yes. That time we got lucky. It turned out an aunt and uncle thought they could do a better job of raising the girls than a single mother."

It seemed unthinkable to Jessie. She couldn't imagine how anyone could purposely put a close relative through the agony of losing a child.

Shaking off the disturbing thoughts, she said, "So he's as good as they say." It wasn't a question but a statement of fact.

"Better. He has a gift for finding people who are lost." Victoria leaned back in her chair, her eyes taking on a new intensity. "I'm good at what I do, Jessie. But I can't touch Cooper when it comes to a missing-person case." In a lighter tone, she added, "Of course, if you ever tell Cooper I said that, I'll deny it emphatically."

Jessie laughed. She really liked this woman. Under different circumstances, another time and place perhaps, Jessie thought they could be friends.

"Ready to go?" Victoria asked.

"Sure." She pushed back her chair and stood. "Do you think Cooper will be back yet?"

Victoria glanced at her watch. "He's been gone nearly two hours. Maybe." Then she shrugged and added, "But then, it depends on what Judge Whitlock wanted."

And what he decides to tell Cooper, Jessie thought.

COOPER TOOK HIS TIME descending the long staircase to where Whitlock and Hal Framen stood watching him. "Sergeant," he said, before either of the other two men could say anything. "Funny running into you again. It must be my lucky day."

"Again?" Whitlock turned toward Hal.

"Cooper was at the hotel with Miss Burkett when she discovered her room had been ransacked," Hal answered.

Whitlock nodded. "Of course." Smiling tightly, he turned back toward Cooper. "Please tell Jessie that if there is anything I can do to help, she should call."

"I'll tell her."

"So what are you doing here, Cooper?" Hal asked.

"I could ask you the same question."

"Mr. Cooper is here at my invitation," Whitlock said to Hal, his voice carrying a warning. "But I believe he's just about finished. Am I right, Mr. Cooper?"

"Not quite." Cooper slipped his hands into his pockets and smiled. "Rosa has been very helpful, and she was just about to introduce me to the rest of the staff."

"What the hell—" Framen began, but Whitlock stopped him with a sharp look.

"Well then," the judge said, "don't let us keep you."

Cooper turned toward Rosa. "Shall we?"

He followed her out of the room, very aware of the two sets of angry eyes directed at his back. The prickly sensation would have normally had him diving for cover. Fighting his instincts, he didn't even glance back.

As Rosa led him toward the back of the house, he sorted through what he knew and what he only suspected.

Hal Framen was the officer working on Nicole Whitlock's disappearance. It was conceivable, even probable, that he'd be here talking to her husband, gathering information just as Cooper was doing. And if Cooper hadn't heard Hal and Whitlock arguing, he might have bought it. But cops *did not* argue with judges. Not a judge like Robert Whitlock, who could crush a man's career with a single phone call. Unless the cop and judge knew each other a whole lot better than anyone would have guessed Hal Framen and Robert Whitlock knew each other.

Cooper smiled to himself.

Things were starting to get interesting. He'd just begun shaking things up a bit, and already cockroaches were scrambling out of the walls.

A half hour later, Cooper didn't feel quite so optimistic.

Interviewing the staff had been useless. If any of the three women knew anything, they weren't talking. He'd spoken to each one individually, but they had the same story, the same answers. Yes, Judge and Mrs. Whitlock had a wonderful marriage. Perfect. Yes, she was young and beautiful and adored her husband. No, they never fought. No, no one had noticed any strangers around lately. No, Mrs. Whitlock had not changed her habits. She hadn't seemed upset or frightened or different in any way lately. Everything was perfect.

Except for one fact: Nicole Whitlock had disappeared. And they were all very sorry about that.

Climbing into his car, he slammed the door shut. It would have been too easy for a member of Whitlock's staff to slip with an important fact. Even the police would have picked up on something like that.

Well, he thought as he started the car, he had Nicole's books and a lot of suspicions.

Now it was time to deal with Jessie. Time to find out just how much of her story had been true and how much was lies.

"YOU DON'T HAVE TO STAY with me all afternoon," Jessie said, as she and Victoria rode the elevators from the top floor. "I'm sure you have work to do. I can sit in the reception area, read a magazine or something and wait for Cooper."

The elevator doors opened, and Victoria stepped out. "You're not getting out of my sight."

"Victoria, I'm not going anywhere."

"That's right. Because I wouldn't want to face Cooper if I lost you."

Shaking her head, Jessie laughed lightly and followed Victoria into her office. "You know," she said, taking a close look at the tastefully appointed room, "I really didn't notice before, but this is very impressive."

"If you want high-paying clients..." Victoria moved toward a grouping of expensive leather furniture

"...it has to look like you're worth it." She settled onto the couch with a satisfied smile.

Jessie took a seat in one of the chairs. "Well, you've succeeded in looking the part."

"Thanks to Cooper."

"Is this another secret you won't admit telling me?" Jessie teased.

Victoria laughed. "No. This one he's very much aware of. Oh, and don't get me wrong. I earned every bit of my success. But this is a tough business for a woman. No one believes you could possibly be any good."

"But Cooper believed in you." Somehow Jessie knew he wouldn't let gender bias get in the way of evaluating someone's ability to do a job.

"We'd worked together, remember? So when he left the FBI, he came to me with an offer. He wanted to work alone, but he needed a place to hang his license and staff to take care of his paperwork and calls. And he knew there would be times when he'd need another investigator or two."

"And you had what he needed?"

"My agency was small stuff...." She laughed abruptly and shook her head. "Let me rephrase that. I was just barely scraping by. But, yes, I had what he needed. An office. A secretary. And my skills."

"Sounds like a match made in heaven."

"Well, I don't know about that." Victoria smiled, and suddenly Jessie found herself wondering about Victoria's relationship with Cooper.

She was an attractive woman, with dark, wide set eyes and a full mouth. If not for Victoria's no-nonsense manner, Jessie would have described her as sultry. Besides that, she was in the same business as Cooper, and from all accounts, good at her job. Jessie could see how a man like Cooper would find Victoria attractive. Maybe there was more to their relationship than appeared on the surface.

Jessie pushed the thought aside. It was none of her business. And why should she care, anyway? Cooper was nothing to her.

"It worked out great for both of us," Victoria said after a moment. "He picked up half my office expenses, but more importantly, he lent my agency credibility. There was a man's name on my door." She shook her head, the look in her eyes revealing how inconceivable she still found the whole thing. "You wouldn't believe the difference it made. Suddenly, I was legit."

"So how long have you been in this office?" It wasn't the question Jessie wanted to ask, but it was safer than what she really wanted to know.

"A couple of years," Victoria answered. "And when we moved, Cooper's name came off the door. At his request. But by that time I had several men working for me, and I'd gained a reputation. I didn't need his name. He still pays half the office expenses, and I supply the manpower whenever he needs an extra hand."

Suddenly Jessie realized that she envied Victoria. She envied her her time with Cooper, her familiarity and easiness with the man. What would it take to be comfortable around someone like him? Jessie didn't know, but suddenly she wanted to very badly.

"Jessie." Startled, she turned toward the door. As if hearing her thoughts, Cooper loomed in the doorway. "We need to talk. Now."

8

BOTH JESSIE AND VICTORIA stood.

"In my office." Cooper started to turn, but stopped when Victoria stepped in front of Jessie.

"What's this about?" his associate asked.

So that was the way of it. Jessie had managed to pull the wool over Vicki's eyes, too, a feat he hadn't thought possible. Victoria Fernandez was the best judge of character he knew.

Well, this time she could very well be wrong.

Meeting her gaze head-on, he said, "I need to speak to Jessie alone. I thought my office would be the best place for all concerned. But if you'd rather we go somewhere else . . ."

Victoria planted her hands on her hips. "I'm not suggesting you go somewhere else. I want to know why you look ready to take someone's head off."

"That's okay, Victoria." Jessie placed a hand on the other woman's arm and smiled reassuringly. Then she turned back to meet Cooper's gaze, her eyes cautious but steady. "I know what he wants to talk about."

A band of anger tightened in Cooper's chest. He hadn't realized until that moment how much he'd wanted—no, counted on—Jessie telling him that

Whitlock had lied. Evidently, that wasn't going to happen.

Knowing she would follow, he turned and walked out. He waited for her in the office he rarely used, standing in front of the window, staring at a skyline he barely saw. When she entered the room, he felt her presence behind him like a brush of warm air. But it wasn't until he heard the soft click of the door closing that he spoke.

"Why didn't you tell me?"

When she didn't answer, he spun around.

She stood ramrod straight in the middle of his office, no trace of an apology on her features. "I didn't think it was important."

"Not important?"

"It has nothing to do with Nicole's disappearance."

"You came to me yesterday, accusing Robert Whitlock of harming his wife." He paused, letting his words sink in. "And you don't think it was important to mention that you'd been engaged to the man?" He took a step toward her. "That he'd jilted you to marry your sister?"

She didn't flinch. Holding her ground, she lifted her chin to silently meet his gaze. He had to hand it to her; she had guts.

"Damn!" Burrowing his fingers through his hair, he swung back to the windows. The woman had lied to him, for God's sake, and here he was admiring her courage.

"You're overreacting," she said.

"Overreacting?" He swiveled back to face her. "I'll tell you about overreacting. Overreacting is being so bitter and angry at your ex-fiancé for ditching you that you accuse him of murder and kidnapping. That, lady, is overreacting."

This time his words struck home. She took a step back, grabbing the top of a chair as if to steady herself. "I was afraid that was how you'd see it."

"You're damn right that's how I see it. And so would the police, or any other investigator with half a brain."

"That's why I couldn't tell you." The simple statement, spoken in that honeyed voice of hers, stopped him.

She was right.

If she'd told him the whole story yesterday, Cooper would be halfway to the Bahamas by now. Even with what she *had* told him, he hadn't bought it until—

"You said that you thought Nicole was running from something," she said, before he could take his own thoughts further. "That there are people, *men*, after her." She took a step toward him, and he could see the effort her next words cost her. "Maybe I was wrong about Robert. Maybe I was wrong about a lot of things." She paused, and he realized he'd never heard her doubt herself before. He wasn't sure he liked it. "But one thing I know for sure," she said. "Nicole needs help."

Cooper again ran a hand through his hair. He was an idiot. The world's biggest sucker. But he was going to see this through. If Nicole Whitlock was still alive, he was her best shot at staying that way. He couldn't turn his back on her, no more than he could turn his back on her sister. On Jessie. Somehow she'd gotten past his defenses, and until this was all over, he couldn't walk away. No matter how much he wanted to. No matter how much it would cost him in the end.

"You weren't wrong about Whitlock," he said finally. "I'm not sure how, but somehow he's involved in all this."

She closed her eyes and nodded.

"Did you love him?" The question slipped out before he even realized he'd thought it. But he couldn't take it back. A part of him needed to hear her answer.

For a moment, she didn't respond, but met his gaze with those dark, turbulent eyes of hers. "Once," she said finally. "I thought I did."

She turned away from him and sank into one of the nearby chairs. "Maybe I was looking for what he gave to Nicole, what everyone, including me, has always given her. Maybe I wanted someone to take care of me for a change." She lowered her gaze to her hands. "But it would never have worked. I never could have been the wife Robert expected. I would have hated it."

Cooper released the breath he hadn't realized he'd been holding. He hadn't liked the idea of Jessie still caring for Robert Whitlock. Hell, he didn't like the idea of her having ever cared for him, period.

"So why did you try to sabotage your sister's marriage?" He asked the question almost as an afterthought.

She lifted her head sharply. "Is that what Robert told you? That I tried to interfere with their marriage?"

"He said you and Nicole argued about it constantly."

Her eyes flashed. "Nicole and I hardly ever argued."

"But *you* were against their marriage. You told me that yourself."

"Only at first. I thought Robert was too old for her. I wanted her to meet someone her own age. I wanted her . . ." again she paused and glanced at her hands, before lifting her gaze back to his ". . . to fall in love."

Cooper wondered if she was talking about Nicole or herself. It was an odd thought, and he couldn't have said where it had come from. But he wanted nothing to do with it. Pushing it aside, he said, "You didn't tell her to leave him?"

"Only the last time we talked, the time I told you about. She sounded so frightened, and I told her to come to Chicago until things settled down. Under other circumstances I never would have suggested she leave him. I knew she loved him."

"And the arguments?"

"Like I told you, we argued over Robert that last night. I was afraid for her."

He paused a moment, watching her face. "Are you telling me everything this time, Jessie?"

She met his gaze with unwavering eyes. "I'm telling you the truth."

Turning away from her, he walked over to look out once again at the city. He believed her. God help him, he believed her. But that didn't mean he was about to trust her. He'd learned long ago how easily trust could be turned back on you. How it could betray you, leaving you torn and bleeding. He wasn't about to make that mistake with Jessie Burkett.

Shifting back to face her, he said, "We've wasted enough time. We have work to do." He started toward the door, stopping to look at her just before stepping out into the hall. "You coming?"

She stood up, looking a bit stunned. "Where?"

"I got a whole list of people who knew your sister."

"You trust me enough to take me with you?"

"Lady, I don't trust you as far as I can throw you, but I'm stuck with you. And I'm not letting you out of my sight."

UNFORTUNATELY, CRYING wasn't an option.

Not now. Not with Cooper sitting beside her in his

flashy black car. Not after she'd lied to him and bullied him into taking her along. Not after telling him she could help, that she knew Nicole better than anyone. And definitely not after finding out that she knew nothing, absolutely nothing at all about her sister.

They'd just spent the last four hours talking to people who'd known Nicole. They'd painted a picture of her that was vastly different from the sister Jessie thought she knew. From all accounts Nicole had become a frivolous socialite whose primary concerns were her hair, nails and what to wear to the next blacktie event she would attend with her powerful husband.

Cooper parked the car again in the underground lot, and Jessie followed him silently up to his office. Once inside, she folded herself into one of his soft leather chairs, wishing for some time alone.

"I know that was hard on you," he said.

She tried to smile but failed miserably. "I'm just tired." Tears would be so easy now. So frighteningly easy. Instead she attempted to make light of it. "Did we learn anything valuable? Besides the fact that Nicole has her nails done on Thursdays and her hair on Fridays?"

Cooper looked at her for a moment before answering, as if gauging her reaction to all this. "It's hard to say," he said finally. Moving behind his desk, he slipped out of his jacket and hung it on the back of his chair. "Sometimes you get seemingly useless information. Then a single piece falls into place, making everything else fit. I'll keep asking questions. Something will click."

Jessie's eyes strayed to his shoulder holster and the gun she'd forgotten he carried. Noticing the direction of her gaze, Cooper slipped the weapon out of the holster and put it in a drawer.

"Better?" he asked.

She nodded, his thoughtful gesture drawing her emotions ever closer to the surface. She didn't want him to be nice to her now. She wanted him to be his usual overbearing self, so she could rant and rave and release some of the anger she felt at Nicole. But he didn't say a word, not even a gesture to indicate that she'd been wrong about her sister. That Jessie didn't know her at all.

Jessie should have stayed behind and let him do his job.

"You were right this morning," she said. "I *haven't* been much help. And I obviously don't know my sister."

"You've had a tough couple of days."

Jessie let out a short laugh. That was the understatement of the year. Resting her head against the back of the chair, she closed her eyes for a moment. Nothing had been easy since that last call from Nicole. And now this. What had happened? What or who had so drastically changed her sister?

"You need something to take your mind off Nicole for a few hours," he said.

"It's a nice thought." Though she doubted it was possible. And what she really needed was a meal, a hot shower, a bed and to be left alone. Not necessarily in that order.

"Come on, let's go find Victoria." Cooper moved back around to the front of the desk. "She's going to take you back up to the condo."

Jessie lifted her head. "Aren't you coming?"

"Our tail will be watching for a man and a woman in a Porsche." Cooper headed for the door, talking as he went. "They won't be expecting the two of you in Victoria's car." Reluctantly, Jessie followed him. "What about you?"

"Don't worry about me." He led her into Victoria's office. "I'll be right behind you. You ready, Vicki?"

She looked up from her desk. "If you are." Evidently they had this all arranged.

"She's ready," he answered. Then, turning back to Jessie, he said, "When you get back to the condo, put on a pair of jeans and a long-sleeved shirt. And if you have it, bring a light jacket."

"For what?"

He ignored her question. "I'll be about a half hour behind you. I'll call from the lobby." With that, he was out the door.

Jessie met Victoria's gaze. He'd done it to them again.

As he'd promised, Cooper called a half hour after Victoria had escorted Jessie into the condo.

"You ready?" he asked when she picked up the receiver.

"Yes. But—"

"Come downstairs then." The phone went dead.

Jessie stood for a moment, staring at the receiver. As usual, Cooper was giving orders. This time, though, she didn't have the energy to fight him. With a sigh, she hung up the phone and headed out the door.

She found him leaning against a wall near the front door, wearing jeans and a black T-shirt, and the sight of him took her breath away.

It was his clothes, she decided. There was something decadent about the fit of his jeans, snug and well-worn, and the way his T-shirt hugged the hard lines of his chest, the color setting off the wind-tossed blond of his hair and the wild blue of his eyes. Dressed like that, there was nothing to hide the real man. Nothing to mask the power and danger of him.

"Come on." Pushing himself away from the wall, he led her out the door toward the biggest, blackest motorcycle she'd ever seen.

"Ever ridden?" he asked.

She shook her head, unable to take her eyes from the machine. "Never." Her father had forbidden it, and even after his death, she'd obeyed his wishes.

"You're in for a treat." Cooper threw one long muscular leg over the seat and handed her a helmet. "Climb on."

Jessie hesitated. "Is it safe?"

He met her gaze, challenging her with his eyes. "Is anything?"

No. Hadn't she found that out today? Not even memories were safe. Still, she wasn't quite ready to throw caution to the wind. "Just how many vehicles do you own?"

He smiled, as if understanding her delay tactics. "Three. The Porsche for show, the Taurus for work and this—" he started the engine, revved it once for emphasis "—is for me." Unhooking his helmet from the handlebars, he slipped it on and then held out his hand to her. "Are you coming?"

Tempted, she took a step toward him.

She had to admit the sight of him on that machine thrilled her. She wanted to be a part of it, a part of something wild and forbidden, if only for a few hours. Putting on the helmet, she took his hand and awkwardly climbed on behind him.

"Hang on," he called as they started moving. "And don't fight me."

He handled the bike effortlessly, and she soon caught the rhythm of riding with him. She learned to go with his movements, letting her body flow with his.

They headed north on A1A. The road skirted the ocean, playing hide-and-seek with the beach between long stretches of condominiums and hotels. It seemed like they rode forever, yet not nearly long enough. They stopped to pick up sandwiches and sodas, then went on, heading north again along the ocean.

It was unlike anything Jessie had ever experienced—the wind whipping past her face, carrying the heavy smells of salt and sea, the machine, dark and powerful, humming beneath her with a pulse and life all its own; and the man, Cooper, his broad back pressing against her breasts, his firm stomach beneath her hands and his thighs hard between hers.

Finally, he pulled the bike off the road, dodging a barricade to stop in a small parking lot on the ocean side of the road. He shut off the engine, and for a moment the silence was deafening. Then the swish of the waves against the sand crept into her awareness.

Cooper pulled off his helmet and ran a hand through his hair. Then he shifted on the narrow seat to look at her. "Ever walk on the beach?"

"Not this beach."

He smiled, and she caught her breath. He was incredibly handsome when he smiled. Almost too handsome. And if she could have backed away, she would have. He was too close; their bodies fitted too snugly together.

Cooper moved first, taking her hand and helping her off the bike. Then, without releasing her, he climbed off himself.

"Take off the helmet," he said in a dark whisper.

Her hand moved of its own volition to the strap under her chin and unfastened it. But it was Cooper who reached up and pulled the helmet from her head, dropping it to the ground.

For a moment she couldn't breathe.

He was going to kiss her. She could see it in his eyes, in the way his gaze dropped to her lips, caressing them with a look before touching them. Something deep inside her tightened, only she couldn't have said whether from fear or anticipation. Then abruptly, his eyes turned hard and he backed away, leaving her cold where a moment ago she'd been too warm.

"There's a couple of picnic tables under those trees," he said, as he retrieved her helmet from the ground. "We can eat there."

Shaken, Jessie couldn't follow him over to the table. Not right away. He'd been about to kiss her; she knew she hadn't imagined it. She'd seen desire in his eyes, and something else. Something darker. Then she realized what. Anger. He'd been angry. It didn't make sense. But then so much about Cooper confused her.

She joined him at the table, and for some time they sat facing the ocean, eating their sandwiches in uncomfortable silence. Eventually, the awkwardness faded, cleansed by their surroundings.

It was a beautiful night.

A light breeze stirred the air. The waves sought the shore in slow easy rolls, breaking gently against the sand. And the nearly full moon rose over the horizon, casting a pearly white glow across the water.

"Nothing quite like it," he said into the silence.

Jessie glanced at him.

"The water," he clarified. "Next to being on it, this is the next best thing." He looked at her and smiled slightly, a little self-consciously, perhaps. "When I was a kid I practically lived on the beach. Night and day." He shrugged. "So did most of the kids I knew."

"I didn't realize you grew up down here." It was the first personal thing he'd ever told her.

"Born and raised."

"Do you still have family here?"

"Some." Then, without elaborating, he said, "Let's walk."

He gathered their sandwich wrappings and dropped them in a nearby garbage can. Jessie watched him walk away, feeling as if she'd just had a door slammed in her face. Obviously Sam Cooper's personal life was off-limits. It was probably for the best.

Cooper walked alone down to the water's edge.

He'd thought he could handle it—taking her out on the bike, bringing her to the beach. It was just supposed to be a few hours diversion, something to clear both their heads and to take Jessie's mind off her sister.

He'd been fooling himself.

This woman was getting to him. He'd be an idiot to deny it any longer. At every twist and turn, she broke down more of his defenses. He saw something in her of the self he'd lost years ago. Her strength. Her determination. Her faith in her sister. He wanted to hold her, protect her, shield her from reality.

Yet there was another side of her. A side that stirred his blood. When he'd turned toward her on the bike, he'd seen the excitement in her eyes. The recklessness of the ride had claimed her as surely as it claimed him. In that moment, he'd wanted her more than his next breath. And she would have let him take her. It had been that very rashness that had stopped him. He'd seen that look before. For the moment, he was her hero. But it wouldn't last. When this was all over, she would see the real man, and she'd walk away.

"I hope you don't mind that I took off my shoes?"

Jessie's voice cut into his thoughts, and he turned around. She looked about sixteen, with her jeans rolled halfway up her calves and her tennis shoes dangling from one hand.

"Not if you don't mind if I leave mine on."

Throwing a glance at his boots, she laughed lightly. "It's a deal." Brushing her soft brown curls away from her face, she added, "I'm sorry if I got too personal back there. I didn't mean anything by it."

Cooper felt like a jerk. She'd asked an innocent question, and he'd reacted like she'd breached national security. "Don't worry about it. It's no big deal. My parents are both still alive. The live in West Palm."

She smiled softly, and it tugged at his insides. "Any sisters or brothers?"

He turned, and they started walking near the water's edge where the wet sand made the going easier. "I'm an only child."

"That must have been lonely."

He turned to look at her. "I never thought about it much."

Thankfully, she let it go. He'd never been comfortable talking about himself. Then, after a few minutes of silence, she said, "So, what's the next step in looking for Nicole?"

"More of the same." Bending, he picked up a shell and tossed it into the water. "We still have a dozen names in Nicole's book."

"Is this how it always is? Talking to dozens of strangers?"

"Pretty much. As they say, investigating is ninety-nine percent legwork and one percent pure terror."

"So why do you do it?"

He glanced at her, surprised by the question. No one had asked him before. Hell, he'd never even asked it of himself. "I guess I like puzzles," he said finally. "And I'm good at solving them."

She nodded, evidently accepting his answer.

"You've never told me what you do," he said, shifting the conversation away from himself.

"You never asked." She glanced sideways at him and smiled impishly.

"I'm asking now."

"I own and run a day-care center." His surprise must have shown on his face, because she laughed, a soft throaty laugh that tied him in knots. "What?" she said. "You don't like kids?"

"No, that's not it. Kids are okay." He shrugged and shoved his hands into his pockets. "It's just not what I expected, that's all."

"What did you expect?" she prodded.

He shook his head. "I don't know."

"I opened the center about nine years ago. My father had left a little money. And with Jacob Anderson's help, I was able to finance the rest. Nicole was only sixteen then, but I thought eventually we could run it together."

"But she didn't agree?"

"Oh no, she loved it. She's great with kids."

"So what happened?"

"She married Robert." She laughed lightly. "Now she's attending balls and black-tie dinners. Can you imagine giving up several dozen messy preschoolers for that?" She laughed again, but this time it sounded forced.

"No." Cooper stopped walking. "I can't."

She stopped, too, but didn't look at him. Instead she focused on the silvery horizon. "Do you know what Nicole wanted to be when she grew up?"

Cooper shook his head.

"A nun. Can you imagine?" She glanced at him for a moment, and he could see the amazement on her face. "She never told anyone. That's not true," she corrected. "She told Father once. His reaction was a bit over the edge. Nicole was his beauty, his doll baby. Just like her mother. So Nicole made a joke of it and never mentioned it again. Except to me."

She started walking again. "I guess we've each chosen our own path. And when this is all over, I'll go back to my finger paints and dirty diapers. Nicole will go back to her parties."

Cooper grabbed her arm and spun her around. "What makes you sure that's what she'll want?"

"Didn't you hear what all those people told us today?" Even in the darkness he could see the pain in her dark, luminous eyes. "My sister's turned into a party girl." She pulled her arm from his grasp and took a step back. "Not that I mind, or that it makes any difference to me what she does with her life. It's just that she hid it from me." There was a spark of anger now in her eyes.

"Jessie—" he began, but she cut him off.

"She hid it. As if it would make any difference how I felt about her." Jessie's voice broke, and Cooper lost the struggle to maintain his distance.

"Don't, Jess." He reached out and pulled her into his arms, holding on when she resisted, until she gripped his shirt in her fists and buried her head against his chest. She didn't cry, not this time, but let him hold her as she stood rigidly in his arms.

Then she softened, slowly, subtly. She sank against him, warming to his touch, to the stroke of his fingers against her back. Shifting slightly, he moved his hands up to cradle her face, tilting it up to his. He saw it in her eyes: she'd left Nicole far behind. There was only the two of them.

God help them both, he thought, as he lowered his mouth to claim hers. They were going to need it.

9

NO ONE HAD EVER KISSED Jessie like this before.

Everything that had come before, every touch, every intimacy paled compared to the desire Cooper stirred in her. The taste of his mouth intoxicated. His lips coaxed, his tongue demanded, until she thought she'd melt from the pleasure he offered. The feel of his large, masculine hands holding her face exposed his need and left her reeling. And the smells, of sand and sea and man, drowned her in their potency. The sensations all rolled together, pooled within her, making her ache for more.

She had to get closer.

Working her hands up his chest, she wrapped her arms around his neck. Cooper growled deep in his throat and grabbed her waist, drawing her tighter against his long hard body. Still it wasn't enough. And when he found her bottom, lifting and pressing the apex of her thighs against his arousal, she let out a frustrated moan.

He released her mouth, watching her face as he rubbed his hardened body against her, teasing them both. He nipped at her lips. But when she would have deepened the kiss, he shifted his mouth to her ear.

A sharp whistle split the air. "Hey, man, go for it!"

Jessie started at the rowdy male voice and tried to pull away from Cooper's embrace. He held her tightly, moving one hand to her waist and the other to her head, pressing it against his chest before she could turn to see who'd been watching them.

"Yeah, man," called a second voice. "Let's see ya do her right there in the sand!" A chorus of crude male laughter followed.

"Easy," Cooper whispered in her ear. "It's just some kids getting their kicks." Aloud he said, "Why don't you boys take a walk?" The command in his voice spoke more than any words.

"Hey, we're just having a little fun, man. No need to get hostile." More laughter rippled through the air, though there was a nervous edge to it now.

"Take your fun somewhere else." Again there was no doubt Cooper meant what he said.

Jessie wanted to tell them off herself, but Cooper held her too tightly. It was an oddly comforting feeling, however, letting someone else take care of things for a change.

"Hey, man. We're going. You all have a good time." There was more laughter, but the sounds grew dimmer.

"They're gone," Cooper said after a couple of minutes. "Are you okay?"

She let out a short laugh and rested her forehead against his broad shoulders. "Just embarrassed, that's all."

Cooper chuckled, a low masculine sound of satisfaction. "It could have been worse." She lifted her head to look up at him. "A few minutes more," he explained, "and they'd have gotten their wish."

Heat rushed to her cheeks.

They'd been that close. If he'd drawn her down to the sand, she would have gone willingly. She would still go, if not for a group of rowdy young men roaming the beach somewhere.

"I thought we decided this wasn't a good idea," she teased.

"It's not." He stroked her back, his touch strong and still hungry. "You're a bad influence on me."

Smiling to herself, she tightened her hold on his neck and laid her head against his chest. She could hear his heart, feel it pounding against her cheek. They stood that way for what seemed an eternity, the lapping waves the only sound breaking the silence.

"Well," she said, wondering when she'd become so bold. "there's always the condo."

"Jessie." She looked up at him again, aware of a new wariness in his voice. "We can't go on with this."

Confused, she tried to back away, but he wouldn't allow it.

"Listen to me," he said. "You're my client—"

"No, I'm not," she interrupted. "I can't afford you. Remember?"

He smiled softly and touched her lips with his fingers. "I'm working a case for you." He took a step back, though he still held firmly to her shoulders—as if he were afraid she'd bolt. "Neither one of us can afford this now. It's a distraction. We need to concentrate on finding Nicole."

For several heartbeats, she couldn't speak. Then she asked, "And what about after this is all over? After we find Nicole?"

"I don't know, Jess." He released her and shoved his hands in his pockets. "*You* tell me what happens. You own a day-care center in Chicago. And me—" he let out a short laugh "—I live on a boat."

JESSIE COULDN'T SLEEP.

She tossed and turned, the memory of Cooper's kiss burrowing into her heart, stirring her senses. She remembered his words, his declaration that they needed to concentrate on Nicole. As always, everything he said made sense. Yet it didn't seem to make a difference. Every time she closed her eyes she saw him, felt him, could still taste his lips.

His touch had claimed her soul, his kiss her heart.

She supposed she should be grateful that he hadn't pushed his advantage. But she wasn't. She wanted him. And for once in her life, she didn't care about consequences or what tomorrow would bring. For once she wanted something just for herself.

Finally, she threw back the covers. Without bothering to put on a robe, she crossed the room to the sliding glass doors. As quietly as possible she opened them and stepped out onto the balcony, which extended the length of the apartment. She moved to the edge and leaned against the railing.

From this high up, with the moon lost behind the building, she couldn't see much. On either side of her a line of similar high-rises lined the coast. Each structure threw off a small amount of light that puddled near its base. But due east, out where she knew the ocean waited, she could see only darkness.

Still, the ocean soothed her. She could smell it, sense its vastness even though she couldn't see it. Funny, she would never have guessed that it would have this effect on her. This pull. Like Cooper.

Suddenly she realized she wasn't alone.

Turning, she saw him standing at the other end of the balcony, a shadow within a shadow. In the darkness she couldn't make out his features, but she knew he watched her. For several minutes neither of them spoke or moved. Yet she felt the connection as strongly as if he still touched her.

Then he walked toward her, a dark looming figure that took form and shape as the dim light from her room pooled about him. He stopped just short of touching distance.

"I couldn't sleep," she said.

He remained silent for several more heartbeats. Finally he said, "You should go inside."

"Why?" She forced herself to look away from him, to gaze out into the featureless night. "It's beautiful out here. The weather's perfect—"

"I'm not talking about the weather."

She turned back to look at him. She had no choice. The darkness in his voice drew her. "I'm not afraid of you," she said.

"You should be."

She took a step toward him. One small step, but it was enough. Enough to touch him. Enough to let him know he'd have to be the one to walk away. She wasn't about to make it easy on him. "What could one night hurt?"

"You don't know what you're asking."

"Yes. I do." She wanted to hold him, to absorb the danger and excitement that was Sam Cooper. For once in her life she wanted to do the unexpected. She wanted the forbidden. "I'm asking for one night. A few hours."

Reaching out, she lay a hand on his chest and heard his sharp intake of breath. It gave her courage.

She moved a little closer and brought her other hand up to join the first. He didn't budge as she touched him, running her palms over the solid planes of his chest, tracing each firm muscle through the fabric of his shirt. She raised her gaze to his face and saw raw hunger in his eyes.

He wanted this as much as she did.

Suddenly there was too much material in the way. She wanted to feel his skin, to know its texture and experience its tautness. She grasped the fabric near his waistband to pull it free, but he stopped her. He grabbed her hands, and again her gaze snapped to his.

His eyes warned her to stop.

She ignored the warning and eased the shirt from his jeans, slipping her hands under the thin cotton. Beneath her fingers, his flesh warmed. She let her hands travel the ridges of his chest until she found his hard male nipples. She caught them between her fingertips and plucked them gently.

This time he grabbed both her arms and pulled them from under his shirt. Then he backed her against the wall.

"My turn," he said. He cupped one breast, squeezing it, molding it in his large hand. Then his fingers worked her nipple through her nightgown, rubbing it and rolling it into a hard bud.

Need spiraled within her. A soft moan escaped her lips and Jessie let her head fall forward against his chest. Suddenly, he released her and took a step back.

Bereft of his support, Jessie staggered and grabbed the wall to steady herself. For several moments they faced each other—again just shy of touching distance.

Finally, Jessie turned and stepped through the bedroom doorway, then swung back around. He remained stoically still. She wondered if she had the nerve to go through with this, and what she'd do if he turned away again.

Cooper wished he could move.

He should walk away. Now. Before it was too late and he followed her into that room. Before he totally lost himself to her. But then, maybe it was already too late. Maybe it had been too late when he'd kissed her tonight on the beach, or last night when he'd wanted nothing more than to comfort her. Possibly it had been too late the first time her voice had curled around his insides, when she'd shown up at his boat.

He watched as her hands dropped to the bottom of her nightgown, paused for the space of a heartbeat and then pulled it over her head. Tossing it aside, she stood in nothing but a wisp of white lace panties.

She was beautiful.

Her small body was perfectly formed, flawlessly proportioned, with long slender legs, a narrow waist and breasts begging to be kissed. Her nipples hardened even as he thought it, and he saw her slight intake of breath.

He brought his gaze back to her face, to the bright flush of her cheeks and the question in her dark eyes. She looked ready to bolt. Yet she stood there, offering herself to him.

It shattered the last of his defenses.

Before realizing it, he'd stepped into the room and lifted her into his arms. She clung to him, burying her face against his chest as he carried her to the bed. Laying her down, he sat beside her, drinking in the sight of her.

"Just one night," she said.

In answer he reached out and touched her cheek, then let his hand drift downward, to the soft swell of her breast. Gently, he brushed the backs of his fingers against one taut nipple and then the other. She closed her eyes, and a soft sigh escaped her lips.

"So perfect," he whispered.

He filled his hands with her, with the creamy skin of her breasts and the dark dusky pink of her nipples. Then he needed to taste her. Leaning forward, he took one tight bud in his mouth, flicking it with his tongue, sucking the tip until she arched against him.

Releasing her, he sat back and moved his hand lower, letting it rest on the flat of her stomach at the top of her lace panties.

She caressed his thigh. "Cooper?"

"Not yet." He stilled her hand. "If you touch me, it'll be over before we've started." He took hold of her other wrist as well, and with one hand pinned them both above her head. "And I want this to last a long time."

Shifting, he stretched out on his side beside her. For a moment he just looked, admiring the proud upthrust of her breasts and her slightly elevated hips. She was a woman waiting to be loved.

He again sought her breasts, first one and then the other, teasing each until she gasped aloud. Then he slid his hand down her body and cupped her mound. Slipping his middle finger into the crease between her thighs, he pushed the silky fabric of her panties against her tender flesh. She groaned and moved against his hand, her legs parting to give him better access. Even through the silk, he could feel the moisture that told him of her readiness.

He lifted his gaze to hers, wanting to see her face as he made her climax. He pressed harder, sliding his finger back and forth, watching as her eyelids fluttered closed, her breath coming in little pants. He covered her mouth with his, absorbing her low throaty moans, his own need straining against the stiff denim of his jeans. Her hips moved harder, and he shifted his hand, this time slipping beneath the lace to touch her directly for the first time.

That's all it took. Convulsing against his fingertips, she pulled her arms free and wrapped them around his shoulders. Digging her nails into his back, she cried aloud, taking a piece of his soul with her.

JESSIE RETURNED to herself slowly.

Little things crept into her awareness. The ocean breeze drifting through the open balcony doors, brushing the sheer curtains against the foot of the bed.

The overhead fan, swishing in its slow, easy cycle. And the feel of Cooper's strong arms, holding her as the last rippling waves of pleasure faded. When she opened her eyes, she saw him watching her, saw the stark hunger in his eyes.

"Take off your clothes," she whispered.

He kissed her, one long, hard, searing kiss, and rolled off the bed. Jessie propped herself up on her arms, watching him as he'd watched her, while he undressed.

Stripping off his shirt, he tossed it aside. Seeing his broad chest, she remembered the feel of it beneath her fingers and ached to touch him again. His hands stilled at the top of his jeans, his gaze finding hers before he slipped his hand into his back pocket, pulled out his wallet and removed a small foil package. Then he unfastened the button, followed by the zipper, and stepped out of his jeans and briefs.

For a moment, the sight of him frightened her.

She realized with blinding clarity that she was about to give herself to a man steeped in danger. In another time, he would have been a warrior. Proud. Fierce. Intensely male. And as much as she wanted this, it terrified her as well. Making love to him would change her, and she'd never be the same again.

Then she looked into his eyes, and her fear evaporated. She wanted him. And for now, nothing else mattered.

He understood her unspoken invitation, because he came to her and, reaching down, slipped his hands under the lace of her panties and drew them off. Jessie fell back against the pillows, a fresh swirl of desire stirring within her. Kneeling between her legs, he lowered himself to her, teasing her with his arousal. She touched his chest with her palms and fingers, reacquainting herself with his hard muscles and crisp hair. Then she shifted her hands to his muscular bottom and urged him toward her. He resisted for a moment, his gaze never leaving hers, and then entered her with a hard thrust.

She watched his face, his eyes as he drove them both over the edge. She'd been right, she thought as pleasure coursed once again through her body. Nothing would ever be the same for her again.

ROBERT PACED the sparsely furnished office.

He'd overstepped his bounds coming here unannounced, unsummoned. But things were getting out of hand, and he wouldn't be treated like an underling any longer. Not even by the Colonel.

After all, what could the man do? Kill him?

Yes. The answer whispered through his thoughts, sending an icy chill down his spine.

"Sloppy work today."

Robert spun around. The Colonel stood inside the doorway.

"Amateur stuff," he said, stepping farther into the room and closing the door behind him. "The way your men went through the Burkett woman's room."

"They were looking for something that might help locate my wife."

"I told you, Cooper will find your wife." The Colonel moved to his desk and seated himself slowly in the chair. "All you need do is get out of his way."

"I tried to hire him."

"There's no need to hire him. Just follow him." The Colonel nodded toward the metal chair in front of his desk. "Sit."

Robert obeyed, attempting to get comfortable by loosening his tie.

"So why are you here?" the Colonel asked.

Remembering his earlier resolve, Robert sat a little straighter and forced himself to meet the Colonel's gaze. "Things are getting out of hand. Cooper's asking too many questions. I don't trust him."

"Of course not."

Robert hesitated, gathering his courage. "I think we should disband. For now, anyway. Until this all blows over."

"No."

"There are too many problems."

"The only problem is your wife. And that will be taken care of as soon as Cooper finds her."

"Look—" Robert scooted forward in his chair "—there's no need to harm Nicole. I can handle her."

"Just like you handled her the night she took off?"

Robert surged to his feet. "She ran because of you. If you hadn't threatened her . . ."

The Colonel stood as well, slowly, every controlled movement a threat. "I think you've said enough."

Not nearly enough, Robert thought. After all, what could be worse than what this man and his organization had already done to him? Or what they would do to Nicole if they found her?

"For God's sake, man, she's my wife."

"God has nothing to do with this. And it's your own life you should be worried about."

10

COOPER WOKE WELL BEFORE dawn.

Instead of getting up, he lay watching Jessie sleep. She looked so peaceful, almost like a child, with her features relaxed and that incredible voice of hers safely silenced for the moment. He reached out to touch her and stopped himself, letting his hand hover above her head. Then he gave in to the temptation and brushed a stray curl off her cheek.

Making love to her had been a mistake.

Yet he didn't regret it. Jessie had been the perfect combination of sweetness and passion. The kind of woman he'd thought he would never find again. The kind of woman he knew better than to get close to.

He needed to rebuild his defenses.

Last night she'd shattered them, taking a part of him he would never get back. He couldn't give her more. He couldn't give her his heart. Not if he wanted to survive when she walked away.

And she *would* walk away.

What she felt for him wasn't real. For the moment, he was her knight in shining armor. But he knew from experience how fast armor tarnished. Once he found Nicole, he'd be just another man. A man she hardly knew, who lived on a boat and hunted down strangers for high-paying attorneys. She'd go back to her school full of children, and he'd be . . .

No. He wasn't going make that mistake again.

He needed to get back to business.

The sooner he found Nicole Whitlock, the sooner he could put this whole mess behind him. Then he would head out to the Caribbean as he'd planned and forget about a certain lady with a voice like heated brandy and a body to match.

With the first streaks of light filtering through the curtains, he slipped out of bed. Grabbing his clothes off the floor, he took one last look at Jessie before heading across the apartment to the second bedroom and shower.

WHEN JESSIE AWOKE, she knew Cooper had gone.

Even before opening her eyes, she felt his absence. Her bed seemed strangely empty, yet today was no different than any other morning. She had been waking up alone for all of her thirty-five years. Just because she'd made love with a man last night didn't mean that things would change. She'd made love before, and life always continued as usual.

That was before Cooper.

It seemed pointless to deny the obvious. Making love to him had changed her. She doubted whether she would ever again be content with her solitary life, with the myriad of other people's children she cared for, or with the string of nice men who'd become her mainstay for an occasional evening out. She wanted more; she wanted a life of her own. She longed to wake up beside the same man every morning, and she yearned to raise her own children. But most of all she needed to again experience the passion she'd felt last night in Cooper's arms.

She rolled over and tentatively touched the indentation on the pillow where he'd lain. A sweet sadness swelled within her. Pulling the pillow toward her, she wrapped her arms around it and hugged it to her chest. It smelled of him. Like the salty ocean breeze, wild and uncontrollable. She'd had a taste of life last night, but instead of satisfying her, it had only whetted her appetite.

She ached for more.

But one night might be all Cooper wanted from her. Just the thought hurt more than she cared to admit. Still, she understood about living with consequences, and she'd known what she was doing when she'd made love to Cooper.

She climbed out of bed and pulled on a robe. It was time to discover what, if anything, last night had meant to him.

She found him on the couch, making notes on a yellow legal pad. Her heart picked up its pace at the sight of him. He wore nothing but a pair of jeans, and her fingers itched to once again run her hands over the hard muscles of his chest.

"Good morning," she said instead.

He looked up and met her gaze, and the memory of what they'd shared flickered briefly in his eyes. "Sleep well?" he asked.

Heat touched her cheeks and she nodded. "You?"

"Yes."

For a moment she didn't know what else to say. She stood there awkwardly, wondering where they stood with each other. She needed to know. "About last night . . ." she began.

He dropped his gaze to the legal pad on his lap and started writing again. After a moment, he said, "Forget it happened, Jessie."

Her stomach churned. "I don't think I can."

He hesitated and then looked up at her. The difference in him from a few moments ago stunned her. All the warmth had left his eyes. "You're going to have to," he said. "I have."

"Just like that?" she demanded.

He shrugged. "You asked for a few hours. A night. That's what you got."

His words struck her like a slap, stunning her. He'd changed guises as quickly and easily as she changed clothes. He'd become the cold, distant man she'd first met a few days ago on his boat. It angered her that he thought he needed to throw this between them as a shield. She wasn't a blushing virgin expecting flowers and promises after spending the night with a man.

"It's time to get back to business," he said, before she could put her thoughts into words. "That is, if you're still interested in finding your sister."

A wave of guilt swept through her—as she knew he'd intended. Still, it worked. She should be thinking about Nicole, not Sam Cooper. And since he'd first shown up on his motorcycle the night before, Jessie had been so focused on him that she'd forgotten her purpose for being here.

Nicole.

Whatever was or wasn't between her and Cooper would have to wait. Moving over to the couch, she sat down, being careful to maintain space between them. "Okay," she said, keeping her voice as even and cool as his. "I imagine the first thing we have to do today is go in and see that police detective."

"Framen will have to wait. I have something else in mind."

"More interviews?"

He looked at her for moment, as if gauging her reaction, and then said, "Actually, I think I've found her."

The unexpected answer jarred her. "Where?"

"At least I know where to look." He paused and then added, "Nuns."

"Nuns?" For several seconds she didn't get it. Then it hit her.

"You told me that someone has always taken care of Nicole," he said. "Why not nuns? Especially since she wanted to become one herself. And you're the only person who knows about it."

It was so simple Jessie wondered why she hadn't thought of it sooner. "It's perfect."

"Almost. We have no idea which order she went to."

"I can start calling around—"

Cooper lifted a hand to cut her off. "It'll take too long," he explained. "No one's going to admit to hiding her, so we'd end up going to every convent in the area. Even then we could easily miss her. We need to narrow the possibilities."

"Okay. But how?"

He thought a moment and then said, "I want to talk to Nicole's housekeeper, Rosa."

"Didn't you question her yesterday?"

"Yes, but something's been bothering me."

"Such as?" she prodded.

"Have you been upstairs in your sister's house, in her study?"

Jessie shook her head. "This is the first time I've been down here since Nicole and Robert married. I've only been to the house twice and didn't go upstairs either time."

"She has a room filled with stuffed animals. Dozens of them."

"Stuffed animals?"

"According to Rosa, Nicole collects them. I take it this isn't a lifelong hobby?"

"She had a teddy bear or two," Jessie said. "Like all kids. But that's it."

"Seems like an odd hobby for a grown woman to acquire. Especially a woman in Nicole's position."

Maybe. But Jessie didn't see the relevance. "What could that have to do with her disappearance?"

Cooper shook his head. "Don't know. But maybe Rosa does."

"Do you think she's hiding something?"

"It's more likely that she doesn't realize what she knows."

Jessie took a deep breath and turned to stare out the floor-to-ceiling windows that overlooked the Atlantic. Could it be this simple to find Nicole? She was almost afraid to hope. "What can I do while you're gone?" she asked, turning back to Cooper.

He rose from the couch, and she tried not to notice the tight fit of his jeans and the top snap, undone.

"Nothing," he said, drawing her gaze back to his face. "You're coming with me."

That surprised her. "What about Robert?"

"Rosa's not working today. We're going to her house. Go put some clothes on." He turned and walked toward the door of the second bedroom.

Jessie stood, suddenly self-conscious in her nightwear. "Why do you want me along?"

Her words stopped him. Turning back to look at her, his gaze swept her from head to toe. "I don't want you, Jessie. But I just might need you."

COOPER FELT LIKE a jerk.

When he'd told Jessie that last night meant nothing to him, it had seemed a good idea. He'd needed to put distance between them. But when he'd seen the hurt and anger in her eyes, it had taken all his willpower to carry through with the charade. It would have been so easy to pull her back into his arms and drag her down onto the couch. They could have made love with the early morning sun streaming through the windows, brushing their bodies with its warmth.

He couldn't do it. Not and walk away from this with his heart intact.

As for taking her with him today, he would have preferred leaving her behind. It would be safer for both of them. But he had a feeling he'd need her help. Rosa hadn't been exactly taken with him yesterday. When he showed up on her doorstep without warning today, he suspected she'd be even less receptive. Jessie might just be his ticket to getting past the housekeeper's reserve.

An hour later they were heading south on I-95 toward Miami.

Rosa lived in an older neighborhood where the homes were smaller but the yards larger than in newer subdivisions. The house itself was typical of South Florida—a one-story, stucco structure with jalousie windows and a huge banyan tree shielding the house from the heaviest of the day's sun.

Cooper pulled into the driveway. Together he and Jessie walked up to the front door and knocked.

When Rosa opened the door, her surprise registered clearly on her features. "Señor Cooper. Señorita Burkett. What are you doing here?"

"Hello, Rosa." Cooper dragged out his best smile, trying to put her at ease. "I'm sorry to bother you on your day off, but I need to ask you a few more questions."

Rosa wasn't buying anything from him—his smile or his questions. "I told you everything I know yesterday."

"This will only take a few minutes," he assured her.

Crossing her arms, she glared at him through the screen door. "Okay. Ask your questions."

Cooper glanced around the small yard, pointedly letting his gaze settle on Rosa's neighbor sitting on the porch next door. "Could we come inside?"

"Ask me here."

"Please, Rosa." Jessie stepped forward, placing a restraining hand on Cooper's arm. "I'm very worried about my sister, and I've hired Mr. Cooper to help find out what happened to her. Please, can't you spare us a few minutes inside?"

Rosa softened marginally. "I'm very sorry about your sister. Señora Whitlock was always very kind to me. But I know nothing that will help you find her."

"There might be something you're unaware of. Please..." Jessie's voice broke, but she quickly regained her composure. "We won't take much of your time."

Rosa hesitated and glanced behind them. "Does Señor Whitlock know you are here?"

"Would that be a problem?" Cooper asked.

She brought her gaze back to his. "He might want to know why you came here instead of asking your questions at his home."

"He won't ever know that we're here."

Again she hesitated, then with obvious reluctance pushed open the screen door. "Come in."

Cooper took a grateful breath and followed the two women into the house. Somehow he knew Rosa held the key to Nicole's whereabouts—if only he could get it from her.

She led them into a small, meticulously kept living room. Motioning toward the couch, she waited for them to sit before taking a seat herself in an armchair facing them. "Now, what do you want to ask me?"

Cooper glanced around, taking special note of the abundance of family pictures. "Nice place," he said.

Rosa obviously wasn't interested in small talk. She simply nodded her acknowledgment of the compliment, folded her hands carefully in her lap and waited.

Cooper had to smile. He may as well get to the point. "Rosa, did Mrs. Whitlock go to church?"

He'd expected the question to surprise her. It didn't. With one brief nod, she said, "With her husband. Every Sunday."

"Where did they go?"

"There's a nondenominational church near their home. Most of the time, that's where they went."

"What about mass?" he asked. "Did they ever go to a Catholic mass?"

Rosa frowned. "They aren't Catholic."

"Nicole's mother was," Jessie explained. "Nicole was raised in the church and used to be fairly religious."

Surprised flitted across Rosa's face. "I didn't know."

"Mrs. Whitlock didn't belong to a particular church or parish then?"

"Not that I knew about."

Even though it was what he'd expected, Cooper wished Rosa could have pointed them in some clear direction. It would have made things easier to find out that Nicole belonged to a parish and had direct contact with a particular religious order. Of course, if finding her were that easy, someone else would have done it already.

"Rosa," he began again, more cautiously now. "Tell me about the stuffed animals. The ones in Mrs. Whitlock's room."

Wariness crept into the woman's eyes. "What about them?"

"You said she collects them."

Rosa shifted and folded her hands in her lap. "Yes."

Cooper picked his words carefully. He'd hit pay dirt, and he didn't want to spook her. "Isn't it unusual for someone of her standing?"

"She is an unusual woman." Rosa sat a little straighter, adjusting the skirt of her dress around her legs. "Very beautiful."

"Rosa," Jessie interjected, "what do you know about the stuffed animals that you're not telling us?"

Jessie's directness threw him, and Cooper held his breath. He had no idea how the older woman would respond. She might just kick them out on their ears. Then again, he hadn't been having any luck with his diplomatic approach. Maybe Jessie had the right idea.

"What difference does it make?" Rosa said, turning toward Jessie. "How can a roomful of toys help you find her?"

"I don't know," Jessie answered. "But I know my sister never collected stuffed animals as a child. And it's not something an adult usually starts. So tell us what you know."

Rosa pursed her lips, obviously trying to decide how much to tell them. Finally, she said, "The stuffed animals changed."

Cooper inched forward in his chair. "What do you mean, they changed?"

Rosa met his gaze. "They were never the same. There were always new ones."

"So her collection kept growing?" he asked.

Rosa shook her head. "One day there would be many. I could not count them all. Then I'd come to work and most of them would be gone. After that she would start bringing new ones home again."

"Did you ever ask her about them?" Jessie asked.

Rosa turned to look at Jessie. "It was not my place."

"But you did wonder," Cooper said.

Again Rosa hesitated, studying her tightly gripped hands. "When my granddaughter Tia was very sick, *señora* gave me one of the largest animals and told me to take it to her. *Señora* said, 'The animals are for the children.'" Rosa lifted her gaze to meet Cooper's. "I never wondered after that."

"She was giving them away?" Cooper said.

Rosa shrugged. "I do not know for sure. But what else could it be?"

"Why keep it a secret?" Jessie asked.

Rosa shook her head. "I do not know."

"And you have no idea who she gave them to?" asked Cooper.

"To children somewhere."

"You never saw her take them out of the house or heard her talk about giving them away?"

Rosa lifted her chin slightly. "I only saw her bring in the new ones."

Cooper believed her. He also believed she'd just handed him the key to finding Jessie's sister, and he suspected she knew it. Standing, he offered her his hand. "Thank you, Rosa. You've been a great help."

To his surprise, she took his hand. "I hope you find her before . . ."

"I'll do my best." He squeezed her hand and turned to Jessie. "Ready?"

"Yes." Jessie stood and smiled warmly at Rosa. "Thank you. I'll tell my sister what a loyal friend you've been."

They started toward the door but stopped when Rosa said, "Señor Cooper?"

He turned back to her. "Yes?"

"Working for Señor Whitlock. It is a good job."

Cooper nodded. "He'll never know we were here."

"Thank you."

Jessie followed him outside. Then she said, "She's afraid of Robert."

"She's afraid of losing her job." He took Jessie's arm and led her down the walk. "She gave us personal information about her employer. To someone like Rosa, that's a betrayal of trust she doesn't take lightly. But she's just given us a vital piece of information."

"The stuffed animals?" Jessie shook her head. "Wherever Nicole is hiding, it can't be the same place where she took those animals."

"There's got to be a connection."

She stopped on the walk and turned to him. "Why? And how can it help us? Most nuns deal with children. You said yourself that it would take weeks to check out all the religious orders in South Florida."

Cooper moved to the car and held the door for her. "We're not talking about children from stable homes. We're talking about children who appreciate something as simple as a stuffed toy."

"So what are you saying? An orphanage? A hospital?" She walked over to him. "I can't believe it. Nicole would never put children in danger."

"Maybe there are other options."

"Like what?"

Suddenly he saw them, halfway down the block. "Don't turn around, Jess," he said, cursing himself for not spotting them sooner. "And keep on talking."

Confusion, understanding and then fear flashed across her features, but she kept her voice low and steady. "What is it?"

"Our friends are back."

11

JESSIE FOUGHT DOWN her panic. "Our friends?"

"In a light-colored sedan, halfway down the block."

Meeting Cooper's gaze, she clung to the steadiness in his eyes. "What happened to the black Cadillac?"

He smiled, a cocky half smile that she figured was half-real and half for show. "Guess they took notes from yours truly."

She forced her own light laugh. "You're sure they're the same men?"

"Sometimes you've got to go with your gut."

It was a sentiment she understood all too well. "What do you want me to do?"

"Keep smiling and get in the car as if nothing's happened."

Nodding, she followed his instructions. Cooper closed her door and circled around to the driver's side.

"Did they follow us from the condo?" she asked once he'd joined her inside the car.

"Maybe." He started the engine "Or they were waiting to pick us up here." He put the car in gear and pulled away from the curb. "Either way, it means I haven't been keeping as far ahead of them as I thought." He glanced at Jessie, and she could almost read his thoughts. He'd been too preoccupied with her. Then, shifting his eyes to the rearview mirror, he said, "Come on, buddy. Let's see if you can keep up."

"You want them to follow us?"

"I'm not crazy about the idea." Again he scanned the rearview mirror. "But it's better than having them hanging around Rosa."

Her stomach tightened in fear for the other woman. "They wouldn't hurt her, would they?"

"They're after us, but I'm not taking any chances." Picking up his cellular phone, he punched the automatic-dial button. After a few moments, he said, "Alice, put Victoria on." A couple of minutes later he spoke again. "Victoria, we've picked up a tail. They may have made the condo." He paused. "Yeah, we're coming in, but we're going to need a way out and a safe place to stay." Another pause. "Good. And get someone down here to keep an eye on Rosa Garcia. The address is 2476 Palm Grove Lane." After a moment, he said, "Thanks," and broke the connection.

"Why are we going back to the office?" Jessie asked.

"I had Alice pick up copies of a Catholic directory that lists all the religious orders in the country. We need to go through the book and look at local orders that work with children, someplace Nicole would feel comfortable hiding." He glanced at Jessie. "It's a long shot, but if we find nuns that meet those qualifications, we may just find her."

"And the men following us?"

"We aren't leading them anywhere they haven't already been." He glanced once more in the rearview mirror. "The trick is going to be getting away from them later."

Jessie settled back in her seat, realizing for the first time how much she'd come to depend on this man. When she'd first contacted him, she'd put Nicole's life in his hands because there had been no other choice. Now Jessie knew she would make the same decision again, only this time she'd do it because she trusted him. If it were humanly possible, Sam Cooper would get them all out of this alive.

When they got back to the office, Victoria had already set things in motion. She had several people going through photocopied pages of the directory, making a list of all the religious orders in South Florida.

Then she, Jessie and Cooper scoured the list, looking for likely locations. They ruled out all the orders that focused on teaching and nursing, and those that ran facilities strictly for the care of children—places where Nicole would endanger the children by being there. It seemed to Jessie like a hopeless task, like trying to pick a winner in a horse race when you didn't know all the players.

Two hours later, Cooper beat the odds.

"Our Lady of Sorrows," he said, reading aloud from the listing. "It's a small order dedicated to women in crisis." He paused and looked up. "They operate a battered women's shelter in Coral Gables."

Victoria reached over and took the directory, reading the entry herself. Then she handed it to Jessie and asked Cooper, "You think this is it?"

"It meets all the criteria," he answered. "Nuns, children, security... Hiding women from men is what they do."

Victoria shook her head. "It's a strong possibility, but it's still a guess. You can't be sure that Nicole even knew about this place."

"She knew about it," Jessie said.

Obviously surprised, both Cooper and Victoria turned to look at her.

Jessie shook her head. "I can't believe I didn't think of it sooner." She paused, realizing she'd had the final piece all along. "It's just been so long."

"What has?" Victoria asked.

Jessie met the other woman's gaze. "For a couple of years, Nicole volunteered at a shelter for battered women. She took care of the children." Jessie paused, remembering one of the biggest fights she'd ever had with her younger sister. "Until I put a stop to it."

Victoria scooted forward in her chair. "Why did you stop her?"

"She was only sixteen. I didn't think it was a healthy environment for a teenager." She took a deep breath. She'd been so young herself, too young to be making life choices for her teenage sister. "She was furious."

"That's when you started the day-care center," Cooper said.

Surprised at his insight, Jessie met his gaze. "I thought as long as she had children to care for she'd be okay."

"I'm surprised they let her near the shelter, she was so young," Victoria said.

Jessie shifted her attention back to Cooper's partner. "They probably wouldn't have, except that Nicole was very close to Ella, the woman who ran the place. We'd met her when we lived with Jacob Anderson and his daughter, Maura, after our parents died. Ella was staying in Jacob's house as well. He was her attorney and offering her protection from her wealthy husband. The man had abused her, and she was suing him for divorce. Later, after the divorce, Ella opened the shelter." Jessie handed the directory back to Victoria. "Our Lady of Sorrows is the place. I'm sure of it."

Cooper turned to Victoria. "Can you get us out of here?"

She walked over to her desk, picked up a set of keys and tossed them to Cooper. "It's a white van, parked on the bottom level and rented under the name Tom Smith."

Cooper pulled out his own keys and gave them to her. "And the safe house?"

She handed him a slip of paper. "It's in West Palm. Here's the address. There's also a second rented car up there. Now give me about a fifteen-minute start and I'll get rid of the goons tailing you."

Cooper turned to Jessie. "Are you ready to go get your sister?"

IT WAS NEARLY DARK by the time they made it back to Coral Gables on the south side of Miami.

Cooper drove past the house once, made a U-turn at the end of the block and then stopped the car several houses away from their destination. For a moment, neither he nor Jessie spoke. Like the houses nearby, the shelter sat well off the road surrounded by a high wall, this one draped in deep purple bougainvillea. There was nothing to indicate that it was anything other than another old-Florida home, graciously restored.

"You'll have to go in alone," he said. "If they see a man, they'll shut down tighter than a clam."

Jessie nodded, keeping her eyes on the incongruously flowered wall.

"If she's in there," Cooper continued, "they're not going to admit it. Even to you."

"I'll get in."

"Jessie..." Cooper touched her arm, and she turned to look at him. "We don't have much time before they find us. They'll figure out pretty quick that Victoria's a decoy. You need to get in and out as quickly as possible. Preferably with Nicole."

"I'll bring her."

He lifted his hand to her cheek, and Jessie trembled at the unexpected warmth that spread through her. Then, hitching her purse strap higher on her shoulder, she pulled away and got out of the car.

The street loomed ahead of her, telescoping, and it seemed to take forever to cross the few hundred yards. She stopped at the front gate and pressed the button near the intercom system.

A few minutes later a disembodied female voice came over the system. "Yes? Can I help you?"

Jessie stepped closer to the speaker. "I need to speak to someone." She heard a whirring sound and looked up to see a surveillance camera slowly scan the area.

"Are you alone?" the voice asked.

"Yes."

A harsh buzz indicated the unlocking of the door-size opening in the gate, and Jessie pushed at the cold, heavy metal. Behind her the door swung back into place with a heavy thunk.

She made her way up the long walkway to the front door. Someone took meticulous care of the yard, and brightly colored impatiens lined the walk. They reminded her of Nicole and the flowers she used to love growing.

On the front porch, Jessie noticed the barred windows and another surveillance camera discreetly placed behind a hanging basket of ivy. She'd come to the right place.

Nicole was here.

Before she could knock, a small nun opened the door. "I'm Sister Frances. May I help you?"

"I hope so." Jessie gripped her hands together around her purse strap. "I'm Jessica Burkett, and I'm looking for my sister, Nicole Whitlock."

"I see," she said, frowning. "I'm afraid I can't help you."

"Please." Jessie stepped closer to the other woman and lowered her voice. "I know this is a shelter for battered women and that Nicole is here." Jessie paused, letting her words sink it. "I must speak to her."

The other woman didn't miss a beat. "I'm sorry. We don't reveal the names of our guests."

"Tell her I'm here then. I'll wait outside."

"I'm sorry." The nun shook her head and started to close the door. "I must ask you to leave."

Jessie slipped her foot between the door and its frame, wedging it firmly. "This is a matter of life or death, Sister. I'm a woman and I'm alone. Let me come in."

"Step away from the door, or I'll have to call the police."

"I'm sorry, Sister." Jessie pushed the door open with surprising strength and propelled herself past the stunned nun. "I need to see Nicole." Hurrying into the house, she ignored the nun's attempts to stop her.

"Nicole!" she yelled, moving from one room to the next.

Upstairs, she heard footsteps scrambling and doors slamming shut, while the small nun tagged along behind, trying to stop her.

"Nicole!" Jessie called again as she headed toward the back of the house, toward the sound of voices.

Suddenly Nicole stepped into a doorway in front of her, bringing Jessie to an abrupt halt.

"You're scaring everyone," her sister said. "Especially the children."

Relief flooded Jessie, and she started to move toward Nicole. Again she stopped, noticing the cluster of small faces in the room behind her. "I'm sorry, I didn't mean to frighten anyone. But I had to find you." She took a small step forward. "I've been so worried."

"You should have stayed away."

Jessie searched Nicole's face, looking for a clue to what was going on here. "I couldn't."

"Why?"

Jessie couldn't believe she had to ask. "You're my sister and I love you. I know you're in some kind of trouble, and I want to help."

Nicole sighed. "I didn't want you involved."

"Involved?" Jessie took another step toward her sister, wishing she could throw her arms around her, but afraid for some reason that Nicole would back away. "Involved in what?"

Just then Cooper burst into the room, with several angry women at his heels. "We got to go, Jess," he said. "Now. We've got company."

ROBERT PRAYED they hadn't found her.

Though he feared God had stopped hearing him the day he'd decided to play God himself. The day he'd met the Colonel and joined his organization.

For the third time in less than a week, Robert sat in the other man's office, waiting. For once, however, he didn't have to wait long. The Colonel joined him almost immediately after Robert had been ushered in. But the look of self-satisfaction on the other man's face crushed what little hope Robert still held.

Hopelessness gave him courage, however. "This had better be important, Colonel. Your man called me out of court."

"We've found your wife."

Robert sank back in his chair, his brief flash of defiance crushed.

"Actually," the Colonel continued, obviously unaware or unconcerned with Robert's distress, "Sam Cooper found her."

"Where?"

"A battered women's shelter in Coral Gables. Rather appropriate, don't you think?" He paused and then added, "I've decided the P.I.'s talent is in his simplicity of thought."

Robert held his tongue, not caring how Cooper had found Nicole.

"My men spotted him and the Burkett woman about a half hour ago." He glanced at his watch. "I suspect by now they've already moved in."

"What are you going to do?"

"Don't worry." The Colonel sat down in his chair, carefully folding his hands on the desk. "They have orders to bring all three of them back alive. That is, unless our talented ex-Fed gives them trouble."

IT HAD JUST BEEN dumb luck that Cooper had spotted them. Either that or the other guys had gotten cocky.

He'd been scanning the area, watching for anything unusual, when he'd suddenly gone on full alert. It had been nothing more than a flare of a match in the near dusk, from a seemingly empty van parked at the end of the block. Suddenly Cooper would have bet his life that the van held something, or someone, other than the flowers advertised on its side.

He hadn't waited to find out for sure.

He'd slipped out of his car and worked his way around to the side of the shelter. Despite the thorny bougainvillea vines, he'd climbed over the wall easily. Getting into the kitchen past a burly delivery man had been a little tougher. The man would have one hell of a headache when he woke up. But pushing his way past several drill sergeants in long black skirts had been the really hard part.

Now he stood in the middle of a group of very angry women. And they were all running out of time.

"Who are you?" Nicole demanded.

"Men aren't allowed in here," one of the nuns said at the same moment. "You'll have to leave."

"It's okay," Jessie said, moving over next to him. "He's with me. He helped me find you."

"I don't care who he's with," Sister Frances said. "Men aren't allowed here under any circumstances."

Jessie turned to Cooper. "What kind of company?"

"Our friends. And they're right behind me." To the nun, he said, "We need to use your back door, Sister. And your car."

The woman bristled.

"Sister, please," Jessie added. "We need to take Nicole and get out of here. The men who are looking for her are dangerous."

"How do we know you're not just as dangerous?"

"I'm her sister." Jessie turned to Nicole. "Tell her!"

"I don't want you involved, Jessie."

"It's too late for that. I *am* involved."

"Look," Cooper said, "we don't have time for this. If I got in here, those men out there are going to find a way in, too. And they're not going to offer any options, nor will they be too picky about who they hurt."

Nicole glared at him. "I had everything under control. You led them here."

"These guys are pros," Cooper said. "They would have found you, anyway. The only difference is you would have been on your own if they'd found you first. Now, are you coming or not?"

Nicole hesitated, glancing from him to Jessie.

Jessie closed the distance between them and took her sister's hands. "You'll put everyone here in danger by staying. Trust me. We have to go."

Nicole threw one more glance at the nun who had spoken, then closed her eyes briefly and nodded. "Okay. Let's go."

Cooper turned to the nun. "We need a car." He reached into his pockets and handed her his keys. "There's a brand-new van parked out front. It's all yours."

The nun hesitated a second longer and looked at Nicole. "Are you sure?"

Nicole nodded. "The men who are looking for me . . . I can't put you all at risk."

"Okay then," she said, glowering at Cooper. "This way."

She led them toward the back of the house. In the kitchen, she took a key off a hook near the door and handed it to Cooper. "It's the old station wagon parked in the alley out the back gate. It's not much, but it runs."

"That's all we need." Pulling his gun from under his jacket, he glanced outside. "And Sister, I suggest you call the police."

"They're already on their way."

He glanced back at her and let out a short laugh. "Yeah, I bet they are." With that, he inched out the door and crouched near the bushes that flanked either side.

The yard looked clear.

Motioning toward Jessie, he said, "Stay close."

Jessie and Nicole followed him across the yard to another iron gate in the back wall. Fortunately, dusk had turned to full night, offering them some cover. At the gate he stopped, glancing around again before opening it and motioning for Nicole and Jessie to wait. Stepping outside, he pressed himself against the wall and scanned the alley.

Again, nothing.

"Okay," he whispered, and Jessie led Nicole into the alley. He motioned toward the car. "Get in the back and lay down."

Jessie nodded, and Cooper carefully closed the gate behind her. He waited until they were safely in the car, then with one final look, started toward the car himself. Then he stopped abruptly as something hard and deadly was pressed into the small of his back.

"Game's up, Cooper. And you lose."

12

"LOSE THE WEAPON," Hal Framen snarled.

Cooper dropped his gun and lifted his hands. "Congratulations. I see the boys in blue got here in record time."

"Oh, we're here all right. Only you aren't going to live long enough to tell about it."

"I'm not dead yet."

Framen pressed the muzzle of his gun a little harder against Cooper's back. "We could remedy that real quick now, couldn't we?"

"You know, Framen, I always figured you were worthless. I just never figured you for stupid as well. So, are you working for Whitlock or what?"

"Shut up. And tell the women to get out of the car."

"Why should I?"

"Because this is a .357 Magnum against the base of your spine, and I've got no qualms about using it."

Cooper shrugged. "You're gonna kill me anyway."

"Yeah, but I know how guys like you think. As long as you're alive, you've still got a chance to be a hero. Now tell them to get out of the car."

Suddenly, the iron gate groaned.

Cooper felt the slight release of pressure as Framen swiveled toward the noise. It was all Cooper needed. A quick half step forward and he swung around, grabbed Framen's wrist and slammed it against the wall, knocking the gun free. Framen went for his throat, but Cooper was quicker, using his weight to shove the cop's body against the wall. His head connected with the hard concrete, once, twice. Then he slumped forward, unconscious, and Cooper stepped back, letting him slide to the ground.

Only then did Cooper look over to see the small nun who'd given him hell inside standing on the other side of the open gate.

"Never did care much for bullies," she said.

Cooper shook his head and smiled. "I owe you, Sister. Now get back inside and lock up before this guy comes around." Grabbing Framen's gun, he jumped into the car. "Stay down and hang on," he said to Jessie and Nicole. "It's gonna be a rough ride."

The old V-8 engine roared to life, and Cooper said a prayer of thanks. Then the car sputtered and choked, and he realized he'd spoken too soon. They would be lucky if the old rattletrap made it more than a couple of miles. And it sure as hell wasn't going to outrun or outmaneuver the men who'd be on their tail any minute. He had to hope that Framen was the only one assigned to case the back of the shelter. Otherwise, this was going to be a very short ride.

Leaving the lights off, Cooper slipped the car into gear and headed for the end of the alley. As he reached the street, he heard sirens in the distance. He silently thanked the vigilant little barracuda of a nun. Cops swarming all over the place might create enough of a diversion for him to get Nicole and Jessie away unnoticed.

That is, if he hadn't just used his last piece of luck.

JESSIE HATED RIDING blind.

Laying flat across the backseat with Nicole crouched on the floor next to her, Jessie fought the urge to sit up and see what was happening. But after a few rough turns with the engine whining and the tires squealing, she decided ignorance was bliss. If they all died inside this hunk of steel, at least she wouldn't see it coming.

Just then Cooper stopped hard, knocking both women against the back of the front seat.

"You okay?" he called.

Jessie couldn't stand it any longer. "What's going on?"

"Nothing more than a little maneuvering."

"Are they following us?"

"Not this time."

"Who is this guy?" Nicole whispered.

"Sam Cooper."

Nicole started to ask another question, but Jessie cut her off. Now wasn't the time to go into long explanation about how she'd found Cooper. There would be time for that later. *If* he got them out of this alive. "It's a long story," she said. "But we can trust him."

Nicole looked doubtful, and Jessie couldn't blame her. Since they had forced their way into the shelter, things had gone from bad to worse. And now Jessie and Nicole were crammed into the back seat of a twenty-year-old car, racing through the streets of Miami, with no idea where they were headed.

"Okay," Cooper said a few minutes later. "I think we're clear now."

Jessie sat up and started to help her sister off the floor.

"I can manage," Nicole said.

Jessie pulled back, stung by her terse words. Nicole had changed, but not in the ways Jessie had been led to expect. Nicole seemed not only determined to do things for herself but angry at her offers of help.

Suddenly, Jessie realized she didn't recognize their surroundings. "Where are we going?"

"The airport," Cooper answered. "We're going to get rid of this car and grab a cab."

"A cab? Are you nuts?" Nicole said. "Those men back there are trying to kill us."

Cooper threw a dark glance over the seat. "In case you didn't notice, Mrs. Whitlock, I just had a .357 Magnum shoved against my spine. I got the idea."

Nicole paled, and Jessie grabbed her hand.

"He knows what he's doing," she said, wondering who she was trying to convince—Nicole or herself.

They made it to the airport without incident, and the transfer went smoothly. They left the station wagon in the longterm parking lot and hiked over to the terminal building.

"If they find the car," Cooper explained, "they'll think we flew out. It might buy us a little time."

"But why don't we do that?" Nicole asked. "Take a flight and get out of Florida?"

"And have them waiting for us on the other end?" Cooper shook his head. "These guys are pros. The minute we use a credit card, it's all over."

They climbed into a cab, and Cooper told the driver to head north. None of them spoke as they left the airport behind.

Exhausted, Jessie closed her eyes and settled back against the hard vinyl seat. She was so grateful to have Nicole sitting beside her. There had been times over the last few weeks when she'd wondered if she would ever see Nicole again. Yet Jessie questioned whether she'd done the right thing. Nicole had been safe until Jessie and Cooper had led those men to the shelter. Now it was anyone's guess what would happen next.

When the cab stopped, Jessie opened her eyes and realized she must have dozed. She climbed out of the car, and the tangy scent of the ocean hit her squarely in the face.

Cooper had taken them to the Fort Lauderdale strip.

A string of shops, small hotels, bars and restaurants, the strip ran along A1A directly across from the public beach. Day or night, the crowds moved up and down the concrete sidewalk. The local youth came to see and be seen, the tourists to take in the native color. Jessie had discovered it the first evening she'd arrived in town, and like every other nonresident, she'd let herself be swept along in the tide of bodies.

This time they fell into the crowds with a purpose, Jessie and Nicole following as Cooper led them south. But he didn't stop as they reached the end of the strip and the crowds thinned. Not until a marina loomed dark and threatening in front of them, did he slow down, and Jessie froze in her tracks.

"No," she said.

Cooper turned and took the few steps back to her. "I'm sorry, Jess." His voice was gentler than she would have expected. "There's no other way."

She searched his face, but in the darkness, she couldn't read his expression. "There has to be."

He touched her cheek briefly and then settled his hands on her shoulders—as if afraid she'd bolt. "Victoria has arranged another safe house for us. But it's in West Palm. That's a good fifty miles north of here."

"Can't we call someone to pick us up or something?" She struggled with her panic. "The police or Victoria? Another cab? Someone?"

He tightened his hold on her shoulders. "That was a cop threatening to put a hole in me back there. I don't know who we can trust. As for Victoria and her people, our friends are keeping too close a watch. Otherwise they never would have tracked us to the shelter." Urgency edged his voice, but there was patience and understanding as well. "Jessie, we need to get up to West Palm on our own. Undetected. And the only way we'll make it is by water."

She wanted desperately to say yes, to be strong. "I don't know if I can."

He slipped his hands up to cradle her face and brought his mouth down to gently brush hers. "I do," he whispered against her lips. "You can do this, Jessie. You're the strongest woman I've ever known."

It was a lie, but it didn't matter. She felt his strength seep into her with his touch, propping her up, giving her courage that she hadn't possessed a moment ago. "Okay," she said. "I'll try."

He smiled, a soft, heart-stopping smile, and kissed her again. Then he wrapped an arm around her shoulder and nodded toward Nicole. Jessie caught the look on her sister's face and knew they had added another question to the dozens they would already have to answer later.

Instead of heading straight for the boat, Cooper led them to a small, one-room shack at the center of the marina. One hard kick to the locked door and it sprang open.

Motioning Jessie and Nicole inside, he said, "Wait here and stay out of sight." Pulling a dollar bill out of his pocket, he pressed it into Jessie's hand. "If I'm not back in fifteen minutes, head to the strip and call the number written on that bill."

"Where are you going?" She didn't want to let him out of her sight.

Again he touched her cheek. "I'll be back, Jess. Trust me." Then he was gone, leaving Jessie and Nicole alone in the dark room, with only the soft whisper of water brushing against the pilings to break the silence. Jessie moved closer to Nicole and reached for her hand. This time Nicole let her take it.

It seemed longer than fifteen minutes when suddenly he reappeared in the doorway. "Let's go," he said without preamble or explanation.

"Cooper," Jessie whispered, realizing how frightened she'd been that he wouldn't return. "Where have—"

He held up a hand to cut her off. "Later, Jess."

She bit back her automatic demand for an explanation. He was right, now wasn't the time. So without another word, she and Nicole followed him outside. They moved quickly, winding their way ever deeper through the labyrinth of wooden docks and water. Finally, he stopped in front of a long, open boat that looked nothing like his graceful sailboat.

"We'd be sitting ducks on the *Freedom Chaser*," he said, answering her unspoken question. "This belongs to a friend." He nodded toward the boat in front of them. "She's built for speed."

He dropped down onto the deck and swiveled back to hold his hand up to her. "Come on, Jess."

She looked at him and then at her sister. Nicole nodded, and Jessie turned back to Cooper. She *did* trust him. And she could do this. Taking his hand, she let him help her down.

"You okay?" he asked.

All she could manage was a nod, but it was enough. He released her and helped Nicole.

"Okay," he said as he began readying the boat. "The best place for you two is in the back." He motioned toward a long cushioned seat that extended across the rear of the boat.

Jessie and Nicole took their seats. And as the low rumble of the engines started beneath them, Jessie waited for the rush of fear to engulf her. Instead, a low thrum of excitement worked its way past the tight knot in her stomach. It was Cooper's doing, she realized. Being with him had changed her in some elemental way. He gave her strength. And courage.

As he eased the boat away from the dock, she kept her eyes on him. Nicole took her hand, and Jessie smiled tightly. She was going to be okay. They left the lights of the marina behind and slipped into the darkness of the Intracoastal Waterway. Still, Cooper took it slow, moving through the dark water without creating a wake. He headed south for a few minutes, under a bridge and toward a wide stretch of water, then turned east toward a break in the land with the open ocean beyond.

"The cut's going to be a little rough," he called back.

She barely heard him. The sight of the open ocean pulled at her, just as it had the night before. For the first time since the day her father had rammed another boat, killing himself and his young wife, Jessie wanted to experience a broad expanse of water beneath her and feel the brush of wind against her face. She'd once loved the water.

But Cooper had been right.

The water grew choppy, and Jessie struggled with a fresh rush of fear. But she kept her eyes on Cooper, on his wide shoulders and his steady handling of the controls, and she got through it. Before she realized it, the water had calmed, and he nosed the boat north.

Then he turned and once again called over his shoulder. "Hold on," he said. "I'm going to open her up."

Jessie nodded and gripped Nicole's hand.

IT TOOK THEM SEVERAL hours to get to the safe house.

The run up the coast was quick and easy, but when Cooper eased up to the dock of a small canal-side bar in West Palm Beach, he ran out of luck. He'd been pulling in favors all night, and had counted on one more friend who owed him to be tending bar. Cooper had planned to slip the guy a few dollars for cab fare in exchange for the use of his car.

It was his friend's night off.

They ended up taking cabs from one night spot to another, working their way west, until they were within a couple miles of the house. They walked the last stretch in a light drizzle.

Jessie and her sister had held up surprisingly well throughout the whole ordeal. Actually, he'd known Jessie would do anything to get her sister to safety— even face her biggest fear. It was Nicole who had surprised him. Everything he'd learned about her had led him to expect a prima donna. But she hadn't lagged behind or spoken a word of complaint since she'd suggested they take a flight out of Miami.

It seemed Jessie wasn't the only strong one in her family.

The safe house, at least, was ready for them. As Cooper checked it out, Jessie and Nicole went in search of dry towels and blankets. By the time he returned to the living room, confident that the house was secure—at least for the night—the smell of coffee filled the air. In the kitchen, he found Jessie filling three mugs. He claimed his, and she carried the other two into the living room, handing one to her sister.

Cooper sat on the chair across from Nicole. "How are you feeling?"

Nicole took a sip of the coffee and nodded. "Better. Thank you."

"Are you ready to tell us what's going on here?" he asked.

She looked surprised. "You don't know?"

Jessie sat next to her sister. "Nicki, all we know is that it has something to do with Robert."

Nicole sighed and put down her cup. "Robert's involved," she said. "But he wouldn't hurt me. I know he wouldn't. But the others..." She shivered and pulled the blanket tighter around her. Jessie slipped an arm around her shoulders.

"What others?" Cooper asked.

"About a month ago I discovered that Robert belonged to a secret organization that call themselves The Regimen. The group is made up of men and women who believe that our legal system is no longer working." She closed her eyes for a moment, then opened them again and looked at Cooper. "They've made themselves the law."

Jessie frowned. "Made themselves the law?"

"Vigilantes?" Cooper asked.

"More or less. Only backed with a lot of money and power. I don't know who all is involved, but I know it extends across the state. There are several high-level judges, county and city politicians, policemen and a man who calls himself the Colonel." She shook her head sadly. "Basically, they decide when justice has not been served, and then mete it out themselves."

Cooper had heard talk of such an organization, vague whisperings. But he'd never paid much attention. In his line of work, there were always rumors. "How did you find out about this?" he asked.

"I found papers in Robert's office that shouldn't have been at the house—criminal files, notes, actual records of meetings with other members of the The Regimen." She shook her head and reached for her cup, her hand trembling slightly. "At first it didn't make sense to me. Probably because I didn't want to believe what I was seeing." She took a sip of coffee and returned her cup to the table.

"Then I confronted Robert, and he admitted his involvement." She looked away, her eyes bright with tears. "He actually believed he was doing the right thing, making the streets safer for children." She brought her gaze back to Cooper, and the tears slipped down her cheek. She was incredibly beautiful, even after all she'd been through in the last few hours. "He's a good man, Mr. Cooper."

Jessie tightened her hold on her sister, but Cooper couldn't lie. "Good men don't try to kill their wives, Nicole."

"It's not Robert who's trying to kill me. It's the Colonel."

Cooper turned back to look at her, the name poking at his memory. "The Colonel?"

"I can identify him. That's why I ran. I'd seen references to him in Robert's paper, but I didn't know his identity."

"Who is he?" Jessie asked.

Nicole looked at her sister, and Cooper could see the fear in her eyes. "I was supposed to be out for the evening," Nicole said. "But I got tired and decided to come home early. I wanted to surprise Robert." She laughed shortly, nervously. "I should have stayed out."

Cooper leaned forward in his chair. "Who is he?"

Nicole turned and met his gaze. "Virgil Raloose. The ex-deputy director of operations for the CIA. I met him once. At a cocktail party in Washington right after he retired."

Dumbfounded, Cooper sank back in his chair. No one would believe him. Hell, he didn't know if he believed it himself. The DDO of the CIA held more power than anyone cared to admit. He had at his beck and call some of the most highly trained operatives in the world. If he were behind this organization, if this was the man they were up against . . .

Cooper shook his head. He needed time to think.

"Okay, get some rest," he said absently. "We'll talk more in the morning." If they were still alive.

13

AN HOUR LATER, Jessie found Cooper on the front patio sitting in the shadows, staring into the distance. There was nothing to see. The house was one of a line of similar houses that faced an empty field, with a wooded area behind it. There were no stars, no moon, nothing but a dark, wet night.

"Can I join you?" she asked.

He looked up at her, but she couldn't make out his expression in the dark. "Sure."

She walked over and sat in the chair next to him. "Not quite as nice as our balcony."

"Welcome to the other part of Florida." His voice dripped with sarcasm. "A few short miles from the Gold Coast and you hit swamp."

But it held its own magic, she thought, as she breathed in the heavy, fetid air. "I always thought of Florida as high-rises and manicured lawns," she said aloud. "But there's more here than that."

She felt him looking at her but kept her own eyes focused straight ahead. She hadn't come out here to talk to him about South Florida. There were other, more pressing matters on her mind. "Did I do the right thing, Cooper?"

This time she did turn, and saw the question on his face. "Should I have left it alone? Let Nicole take care of herself?" Jessie tucked her legs underneath her and wrapped her arms around herself. "I keep thinking if we hadn't barged in there today . . ."

"Jessie, don't." He reached over and claimed one of her hands. "You did what you had to do. The only thing you could have done."

She shook her head. "I'm not so sure. And Nicole obviously doesn't think so." She hesitated, searching for the words that would make him understand. "It's just that I've been mothering Nicole for so long . . . I don't know how *not* to take care of her." Again she paused, thinking of the changes she'd seen in her sister. "Maybe it's time I learned."

"Maybe." He slipped his fingers through hers and tightened his hold. "But in this case, you did the right thing. I meant what I said back at the shelter. Those men may have followed us to Nicole, but they'd have found her sooner or later on their own. And they would have taken her out of that house and killed her."

Jessie closed her eyes briefly and nodded. "I guess you're right." Though she wasn't sure she believed it. Everything she'd done since coming down here to search for Nicole had felt off, somehow. Everything except her involvement with Cooper. It had felt right to make love to him. But that just went to show how wrong she could be.

"You did good tonight, Jess," he said, interrupting her thoughts. "Getting on that boat took guts."

It surprised her that he didn't realize why she'd been able to do it. "I knew you'd keep us safe."

He let out a short laugh that held little humor. "But for how long?" He released her hand and after a few minutes of silence said, "This is way over my head, Jess. I deal with petty crooks, runaways, bail jumpers, even the mob on occasion. But this . . ." He lifted his hands, palms up, and then dropped them again.

She unfolded her legs and shifted sideways in her chair. "You must know people you can go to. People in the FBI?"

"Without any evidence?" He shook his head. "Who's going to believe me? And even if they did, no one's fool enough to go up against a man like Raloose without hard proof."

"What about Nicole? She'll testify against him."

Cooper gave her a grim smile. "If she lives that long." Jessie winced, but Cooper wasn't finished. "And if she does, it will still be her word against a lot of very powerful people."

"What about us? We can back her up."

"Everything we know, or think we know, comes from Nicole."

"And the cop with the gun?"

"Oh, Framen will go down all right. If *he* lives that long. But so what? Whatever his true role is, he's expendable."

Jessie felt his frustration, and it frightened her. Yet in her heart she still believed in him. Reaching over, she lay a hand on his arm. With a start he looked at her, meeting her gaze across the few feet that separated them. She saw in his eyes the moment he realized what she was offering him. Trust. Faith.

Standing, he stepped over to the railing, moving away from her. Away from what she offered. After a few moments, he said, "I didn't mean what I said this morning, Jess. About last night."

Her heart skipped a beat. "I know."

He turned back to her, his gaze drifting over her, hot and hungry. "Another time, another place, perhaps . . ."

Jessie held her breath, unable to speak, waiting for him to close the space between them, willing him to reach out to her. Instead, he swung back around, leaning once more against the porch railing.

"Cooper, why did you leave the Bureau?"

Long minutes passed, and she didn't think he would answer. Then he said, "I was brought up on charges of negligence. I let my personal feelings interfere with an investigation." He faced her again, his body rigid with tension. "Because of it, a little girl died."

She didn't believe it. Couldn't. "No."

"I fell in love with the girl's mother." His voice was hard, bitter, disgusted. "If I hadn't been distracted, preoccupied, that little girl would be alive today."

For a moment Jessie couldn't speak. Then she said, "That's why you turned me away this morning. Why you didn't want to make love last night."

"Go to bed, Jessie." He swung back around, away from her. "It's been a long day."

Jessie sat motionless, her nails digging into the palms of her hands. She ached to step up behind him and slip her arms around his waist. She wanted to lay her head against his broad back and cry. For a lost little girl. For her mother. And for him.

She couldn't do it.

Last night she'd thrown herself at him, all but begged him to make love to her. If there was ever going to be anything between them, this time he'd have to come to her.

Finally, she stood. "This isn't over."

"It never started."

She lifted her hand to him and then pulled it back. "You know where I am if you change your mind."

"Good night, Jessie."

"Good night . . . Sam."

COOPER WISHED HE HAD a cigarette. It didn't matter that he'd quit ten years ago. At times like these, the craving was as fresh and raw as if it had been yesterday. He sat in the dark, his Walther .380 semiautomatic fully loaded on his lap, and thought of Jessie.

He could have lost her today.

He'd been stupid and careless, and they'd all come damn close to being history. Yet she'd hung in there, staying with him every step, even getting on that boat because he'd told her it was the only way. Despite everything, she'd believed in him.

It was more than he deserved.

He'd never known a stronger, more courageous woman. She'd do anything, face any odds to protect someone she loved. He doubted whether Nicole knew how lucky she was. Cooper would give his life to have someone—to have Jessie—care for him like that.

He loved her.

The realization came out of nowhere, but it didn't surprise him. It had been creeping up on him, circling, waiting to claim him since the first day he'd met her. He'd tried to evade it, to keep *her* at a distance. But fate had a twisted sense of humor, and some things were inevitable. Like Sam Cooper falling in love with Jessie Burkett.

Now that they both might end up dead.

He would do his best to protect her, to protect them all. They might last a day or two, or even a week. But eventually, Raloose would find them. Then it would be all over. Cooper realized suddenly that he couldn't go to his grave without touching her one more time.

Putting the gun back in its holster, he slipped into the house. Inside, silence greeted him, but he stood for a moment anyway, listening. Then he crossed to Jessie's room and hesitated with his hand on the doorknob. He could still walk away, he told himself. But he knew it was a lie.

He opened the door.

Jessie sat up in bed with a start. Another step. He set his shoulder holster on the dresser and closed the door behind him.

For a space of a heartbeat, neither of them moved.

Then a small cry escaped her lips, and she flew off the bed. He caught her in midflight, his arms wrapping around her waist, lifting her, pulling her close, his mouth claiming hers in a desperate kiss.

Never again. He might never have her again. The thought tore at him, ripping at his heart, shredding his soul.

Turning, he pressed her against the wall, his hands, his mouth seeking, feeling, memorizing every detail of her sweetness.

Once more. One more time he would have her.

Moaning, she met his need with her own, tearing at his shirt and shoving it off his shoulders, her hands connecting with his skin like hot streaks of fire, her lips following her hands, burning their way into his soul. He gripped her head, holding it against his chest, as if he could make her a part of him.

He couldn't lose her. Not now. He'd just found her.

Reaching underneath her T-shirt, he grabbed her panties and yanked them down. On his knees, he worked his way back up her legs with his mouth, wanting to taste every part of her. Then he gripped her buttocks, holding her close as he found her core and buried his tongue in the sweet crevice between her legs.

With a cry of pleasure, she arched against him.

She was everywhere, everything. Heavy breathing and frantic moans of need. Frenzied hands in his hair, kneading, pulling. Soft skin and trembling buttocks. Swollen, salty need. And the smell of sex, hot and hungry.

He needed her now.

Standing, he fumbled with his belt while she groped at his zipper. Then his sex sprang from his jeans. He lifted her against the wall, her legs wrapped around his waist, and drove into her. For a moment he stilled, tearing his mouth from hers to look into her dark eyes.

And lost himself.

He thrust into her, harder and faster, while she wound her fingers into his hair, her mouth working its way across his face, kissing him, loving him as her body arched against him. Then she cried out, and he followed her over the edge, spilling his heart and soul into hers.

SHE LOVED HIM.

It was more than the sex, more than the danger of him. It was Cooper himself. His strength. His need. His compassion.

After their frantic lovemaking, he carried her to the bed. Laying her down, he sat for a moment next to her, brushing strands of hair from her cheek.

"I'm not going to let them hurt you, Jess," he said.

She smiled tightly, her heart swelling. "I know."

"I have to go now and keep an eye on things."

She nodded, not trusting herself with words. She understood why he couldn't stay with her, but that didn't make her want it any less. He leaned over and brushed his lips against hers. Then he stood, walked to the dresser and picked up his gun before leaving the room.

She fell asleep then, knowing he would protect them.

When she finally made it into the kitchen the next morning, Nicole had coffee brewed and was making breakfast.

"Where's Cooper?" Jessie asked, forcing herself to sit at the table instead of offering to take over the food preparations.

Nicole poured a cup of coffee, brought it over and set it in front of her. "He went to get cleaned up. Seems he didn't sleep last night."

Jessie took a sip of the coffee without commenting. She'd known he would stay up watching, keeping her and her sister safe.

Bringing her own coffee over, Nicole pulled out a chair and sat down. "Where did you find him?"

"Jacob gave me his name."

"He's very resourceful."

Jessie nodded, wary of where Nicole was heading with this.

"So, what's going on between the two of you?" she asked.

Heat burned Jessie's cheeks. "Is it that obvious?"

"He got you on a boat."

Jessie sighed and turned to look out the window. The view wasn't much better in the daytime. The sky was overcast and the field across the street was overgrown with tall, scraggly brush. "I don't think it's going anywhere."

"Why not?"

She shrugged and wrapped her hands around her coffee cup. "I run a day-care center in Chicago," she said, repeating the excuse Cooper had used with her. "And he lives on a boat."

Nicole looked doubtful, but then Jessie didn't buy the explanation herself. There was more standing between her and Cooper than where they lived and what they did for a living. He breathed adventure and danger. She was steady and sensible. Besides, Cooper himself kept putting up roadblocks. He'd been burned once and didn't seem inclined to let it happen again. Oh, he wanted her all right, but lust was a long way from love.

"I sure could use some of that coffee."

The deep male voice surprised her, and Jessie looked up to see Cooper lounging in the doorway. Memories of the night before swept over her in a rush. It was impossible to look at him and not recall the most intimate details.

"There's plenty," Nicole said, rising from her chair. "Sit down and I'll get it for you."

"Thanks." Cooper walked over to the table, and flipping a chair around backward, straddled it. "Morning, Jess."

Jessie smiled, not quite believing how sexy he looked, despite his lack of sleep. "Good morning."

Nicole brought a cup to the table. "Hungry? I made a huge omelet."

Cooper kept his eyes on Jessie a moment longer, then turned and nodded to Nicole. "Sure. Sounds good."

Nicole served the omelet. While eating, they kept the conversation light. In unspoken agreement, they put off dealing with the problems facing them for the space of this one last meal. Eventually they finished, and their short reprieve ended.

"I made some calls this morning," Cooper said without preamble. "I have friends in the Bureau who have offered to protect you both."

Jessie tightened her hands on her cup. "You're going to send us away."

"It's for your own good. You're in danger here."

Jessie pushed herself back from the table. "And you're not?"

"I can take care of myself. Besides—" he glanced at Nicole "—someone needs to expose this organization."

"You can't do this." Jessie crossed her arms and glared at him. "You can't expect me to walk away after everything that's happened."

Cooper turned back to meet her gaze. "I expect you to be sensible for once. Take your sister and—"

"I'm not leaving," Nicole said calmly. "It's my husband you're going after, and I'm not leaving him."

Cooper frowned, obviously frustrated, and pushed out of his chair. "You're both suicidal."

"Believe me, Cooper, I want to live," Nicole said, looking up at him. "But you need me. If you're going to expose The Regimen, I'm the only one who can get you the proof you need."

"She's right," Jessie said, returning to the chair next to her sister. "The papers you saw, right? The ones with details about The Regimen?"

Nicole nodded. "Robert keeps them in his safe."

Jessie looked up at Cooper. "If we got Robert's papers, wouldn't they help your case?"

"Wait a minute." Cooper ran a hand through his hair. "Slow down. What you're suggesting is dangerous."

"We're already in danger, even if we go into hiding. You said yourself it's only a matter of time before they find us. We're not going to be safe until this organization no longer exists," Jessie argued.

She saw the torment in his eyes. "Don't do this!" he pleaded.

"I can't leave."

For what seemed an eternity she held his gaze, refusing to turn away, watching the sweep of emotions rush through him—anger, frustration, determination. She suspected he both wanted her here with him and wanted to send her away.

Finally, he turned to Nicole and said, "Do you know the combination to Robert's safe?"

"He made me memorize it."

Cooper paused a moment and then said, "Okay. We'll try it. We'll only get one shot, though."

"What about Robert?" Jessie asked. "He's not going to let us just walk in there and take what we want."

"We'll have to make sure he's out of the house." Again he thought for a minute before continuing. "Nicole, do you think you could get him to meet you?"

"No—" Jessie began, but Cooper cut her off.

"She won't really meet him. Just call and arrange it." Then to Nicole he said, "Do you think you can convince him?"

Nicole nodded. "Yes. I'm sure of it."

"Okay," Cooper said. "Once he's out of the house, I'll take you two somewhere in the area where you'll be relatively safe. Then I'll move in."

"The safest place for us is with you," Jessie said.

"She's right," Nicole agreed. "Besides, I can get you in and out of the house without anybody looking twice."

Again frustration crossed his features, but then he nodded. Evidently, he'd had to make one last attempt to send them away to safety. In the end he must have realized what Jessie already knew.

They were in this together.

14

No one spoke as they drove back to Fort Lauderdale.

Cooper suspected both Jessie and Nicole were lost in their own fearful thoughts. As for him, he went over and over his strategy in his mind. Everything depended on them getting in and out of Whitlock's house without being detected. Cooper had alerted Victoria, and she had several operatives in the area in case anything went wrong. But that was the only backup Cooper trusted. Without knowing who was involved in The Regimen, they couldn't possibly contact the police. So he tried to think of every contingency, every possible way his plan could go wrong.

He knew better. Things never went as planned. As soon as you forgot that, you were in trouble. He just needed to make damn sure that no matter what happened, Jessie and Nicole made it to safety. That's what Victoria's people were for.

A couple of miles from the house, Cooper stopped at a small diner so Nicole could call Whitlock. As she'd promised, he seemed eager to see her. But Cooper knew that was no guarantee Whitlock wouldn't let someone else know about Nicole's call. Someone like Raloose. Cooper had to trust her when she claimed her husband wouldn't hurt her. It wasn't easy—especially with all the evidence to the contrary.

After arranging the meeting with Whitlock, they drove toward Nicole's house and parked a half block away from the formal entrance to the exclusive neighborhood. When Robert's car passed them on his way to the meeting his wife wouldn't keep, Cooper headed for the house. He pulled far up the drive, hoping the car would be less visible from the street. Within minutes they were inside, and Nicole had shut off the alarm.

"Okay, Jess," Cooper said. "Stay here and keep an eye out. Nicole, come with me."

He led Nicole back to her husband's office. They opened the door, and she immediately went to the keypad and shut off the silent alarm.

"Okay, where is the safe?" Cooper asked.

"Behind the bookcase." She walked over and pressed a button underneath the desk. A small bookcase slid to the side, revealing a walk-in safe.

Cooper whistled softly. "Your husband doesn't fool around."

"He believes in getting the best."

"Good thing he can afford it." Cooper joined her in front of the unit. "Okay, let's get it open."

It took Nicole two tries to get the combinations right, but finally she succeeded. Stepping inside, she retrieved a brown, nondescript accordion file. "This is it."

Cooper took the file to the desk and glanced through the papers. It seemed to be all there, just as Nicole had said—names, records of meetings, decisions made. This file would put a lot of powerful people away for a very long time.

"He's going to prison, isn't he?" Nicole said.

Surprised, Cooper looked up to see that she'd moved over to stand near the windows, her arms wrapped tightly around her waist. He couldn't lie. "Yes."

"He thought he was doing the right thing."

"You and I know that's not the case."

She turned to look at him, tears streaming down her face. "I do love him, you know."

Cooper wished he could say something to comfort her, but the words weren't there. Not for the likes of Robert Whitlock. "We've got to go, Nicole," he said instead.

"Not so fast, Cooper."

Cooper turned toward the door and froze. Whitlock and Framen stood just inside the room. Framen held Jessie, his arm wrapped around her throat, his .357 Magnum at her temple.

"He'll kill her," Whitlock said, nodding toward Framen.

Nicole stepped away from the windows. "Robert, no!"

"Stay back, Nicki. I don't want to hurt her, but I will if I have to."

Fear and rage wrenched at Cooper's gut. "Let her go, Whitlock."

"I don't think so. Not just yet."

Cooper fought down his emotions, and a cold, deadly calm settled over him. "What are you going to do? Kill us all, your wife included?"

"Only if I have to. Now hand over the gun."

Cooper moved his hand to his jacket.

"Careful!" Framen pressed his weapon harder against Jessie's temple.

With deliberate slowness, Cooper withdrew his gun with two fingers and held it out. "So I was right about you, Framen. You're Whitlock's lapdog. And the others, the pros, they must belong to Raloose."

"You talk too much, Cooper," Whitlock snapped. "Drop the gun and kick it over here."

Cooper set his gun on the floor and nudged it with his foot.

"Robert..." Nicole started toward her husband, but stopped abruptly when Framen took a step back, pulling Jessie with him.

"I wouldn't, Mrs. Whitlock," he said. "Your sister here has caused us a lot of trouble. I'd just as soon shoot her as not."

Nicole lifted a hand to her mouth, her eyes wide and brimming with tears. "Let her go. I'm the one you want."

"No, Nicki . . ." Jessie said.

Framen jerked his arm against Jessie's throat, silencing her. "Do I have to gag you, woman? Shut up."

Cooper clamped down on his fury. He was going to make Framen pay for hurting Jessie. Ten minutes alone with him before the cops locked him away for good was all Cooper needed.

Whitlock retrieved Cooper's gun from the floor and backed up next to Framen. "Okay, Cooper, gather up all those papers and put them back in the file."

With deliberate slowness, Cooper complied. "You know, you can't get away with this."

"Please, let's not be trite." Whitlock motioned toward the safe with his gun. "Toward the back wall there's a briefcase. Get it and put it on the desk next to the file."

As Cooper set down the briefcase, he asked, "So what's the deal, Whitlock—you and Framen going to try and run?"

"A man with a Swiss bank account can live anywhere."

"Raloose may not be too happy about that."

"He has to find me first."

Cooper snorted in disgust. "What does a man like you know about disappearing?"

"Money will buy anything. Now, step back into the safe." He waited until Cooper had done what he'd ordered and then nodded toward Framen. "Okay, Hal, let the girl go."

Framen hesitated a moment, but then released Jessie.

She moved over to Cooper, and he wrapped his arms around her briefly, just long enough to know she was okay. Though he could feel her trembling, there were no tears. Again he thought she was one of the bravest women he'd ever known.

"Okay, Nicki," Whitlock said. "Bring me the file and the briefcase."

Nicole moved slowly toward the desk. "Why are you doing this, Robert?"

"That should be obvious. I've no intention of spending the next twenty years in prison." He paused and then said, "Come with me, Nicki."

She stopped and faced him. "I can't."

Whitlock shook his head. "I'm sorry then."

"What are you going to do with us?"

"You'll have a short stay in the safe. It'll be uncomfortable, but you'll survive. As soon as I'm out of the country, I'll call the authorities and let them know where to find you." He nodded toward the desk. "Now bring me the briefcase and file."

Nicole turned and picked them up, but instead of handing them to her husband, she stepped in front of Jessie and Cooper. "You'll have to come get them."

Whitlock's gaze darted to Framen and then back again. "Nicole, you don't know what you're saying."

"All the proof you need is in this file. Turn it over to the district attorney's office, and they'll go easier on you."

"Shut up," Framen snapped. "Bring the briefcase."

"You'll have to shoot me."

Cooper started to step forward to stop her. This wasn't worth dying for. "Nicole—"

"It looks like I got here just in time."

Cooper froze, his gaze snapping to the stranger in the doorway, while Whitlock and Framen spun around, obviously just as surprised. The stakes had just gotten higher, Cooper realized. He had no doubt about the newcomer's identity: Virgil Raloose.

Whitlock spoke first. "Colonel, what are you doing here?"

"Checking up on you, of course." Raloose stepped into the room and took a moment to survey its occupants. Though his stance was casual, Cooper wasn't deceived. The man was dangerous—more dangerous than a dozen Framens or two dozen Whitlocks.

"This is quite a gathering you have here, Judge," Raloose said and glanced toward Framen. "You have your trusty, though incompetent civil servant." The detective's face reddened, but Raloose ignored him. "And your lovely wife." He turned and stepped toward Nicole. "So good to see you again, my dear." He moved his hand to touch her face, but she jerked away from him.

He smiled, a slow, sick smile that turned Cooper's stomach. Then Raloose shifted his malevolent gaze to Cooper and Jessie. "This must be your sister, Jessica. And the illustrious Mr. Cooper." He stood a moment, his gaze locked with Cooper's. "I must say you've given my men quite a chase."

"Glad to hear it."

"I could use a man like you."

"Not a chance."

"Too bad." Raloose turned away and walked back to the doorway, his back to the room. "Nicole, bring me the briefcase and file."

She stiffened and stood a little straighter. "No."

For the space of a heartbeat silence fell over the room, as if no one dared to breath. Then Raloose shifted his hand toward his jacket, and Cooper reacted instinctively, shoving Jessie toward the back of the safe. "Get down, Jess."

"Have it your way," Raloose said, and he turned, gun raised.

Cooper dove for Nicole, throwing her to the floor and rolling with her behind the desk as two shots split the air. Then he went for the .86 Beretta on his ankle and inched around the desk.

Framen had fled and Whitlock stood over Raloose, who was lying on the floor, a bullet wound in his chest. Two quick strides and Cooper disarmed the judge, who looked up at him with a dazed expression.

"He was going to shoot her," Whitlock said.

Cooper looked at him in disgust. "Yeah. That's what happens when you play with guns."

IT HAD BEEN FOUR WEEKS since Jessie had seen Cooper. The first two she understood. The district attorney's office had spirited her and Nicole away to yet another safe house. No one, not even Sam Cooper, was allowed near them. Finally, the indictments were handed down and members of The Regimen arrested.

Robert had been charged along with the others, but he'd agreed to become a state's witness. That, plus the fact that he'd saved Nicole's life at the last minute, promised to help him when it came time for sentencing. Even so, he was looking at years in prison. Virgil Raloose had lived to face charges that would put him away for the rest of his life. Hal Framen had been caught within blocks of the Whitlocks' house, and like Raloose, would spend a great deal of time behind government walls.

Finally, as the last members of The Regimen were rounded up and arrested, the two sisters were allowed to return to Nicole's house. Jessie hung around for another couple of weeks, under the guise of offering support. In truth, she was waiting for Cooper to come for her. Or at least come and tell her goodbye.

He did neither.

As the days passed, her emotions swung from impatience to anger and settled on sadness. She couldn't make him care for her if he didn't. It had to be his choice. But without him, her life yawned before her long and empty. At the end of two weeks, she decided it was time to go home.

Her flight left at one. She'd gotten up early to pack, and was surprised when Victoria showed up, carrying a cup of coffee.

"Nicole sent this up," she said, handing the cup to Jessie. "Hope you don't mind me barging in on you like this."

In truth, Jessie did mind. She wasn't up to talking to anyone. Or saying goodbye. But Victoria had been kind to her. Jessie couldn't repay her with rudeness. "Thanks," she said, taking a sip of the coffee and setting it on the nightstand.

Victoria settled on the corner of the bed, eyeing Jessie's half-filled suitcase. "I take it you're leaving."

"It's time. I have a business to run. A life to get back to." Jessie walked over to the dresser and pulled an armload of clothes from one of the drawers. "Thank you, though, for everything you've done."

"Cooper did all the work."

"Yes, well . . ." Jessie kept her eyes on her packing. "I know you helped."

"Have you spoken to him?"

"Not since the night they arrested Robert."

"Why not?"

A bit of the old anger surfaced, and she shot Victoria a withering look. "Maybe you should ask him that."

"You love him, don't you?"

"What does that have to do with anything?"

"Maybe you should tell him."

"Please, Victoria." Jessie shook her head and moved back to the dresser for more clothes. "If he'd wanted to see me, he knew where I was."

"You're as stubborn as he is."

She dropped another armload of clothes in the suitcase, shoving them down to make them fit. "Leave it alone."

"Did he ever tell you why he left the Bureau?"

Jessie sighed. "He told me he was brought up on charges of negligence."

"Which were dropped."

Jessie crossed her arms and glared at the other woman. "I thought you didn't know why he left."

"I lied."

"Great." Jessie slammed her suitcase shut and clicked the locks into place.

"The woman he was involved with—the one whose daughter they found too late—"

"I don't want to hear this, Victoria."

"She filed a complaint against Cooper."

That stopped Jessie, and she swiveled around to look at Victoria. "She was the reason Cooper was brought up on charges?"

"Cooper already blamed himself. You always do when a case goes bad. But it wasn't his fault. The girl had been dead weeks before the FBI got involved. Still, when her mother accused Cooper . . ." Victoria shrugged, letting her voice trail off.

For a moment Jessie couldn't speak. "But that doesn't make any sense. Everything worked out for us."

"What if it hadn't?"

"It wouldn't have changed how I feel about him."

"As I said before, have you told him that?" Victoria stood and headed for the door. "Think about it."

Jessie collapsed on the bed. Could he possibly not know how she felt about him? Could she leave without being sure?

IT HAD BEEN THE MOST miserable month of Cooper's life.

He hadn't minded helping the authorities with the "Regimen" case. Nor had he cared about the endless hours of searching records for more information on the organization, making sure they had all the pieces, all the players. Finding people was what he did, and he was good at it.

It was Jessie who made him miserable.

Or actually, her absence. No matter how hard he worked, how hard he drove himself, he couldn't seem to get her off his mind. When he closed his eyes at night, he heard her voice. Sometimes he'd spot a woman with big brown eyes and remember the way Jessie had of looking him squarely in the eye, demanding to have her own way.

It was enough to drive him mad.

Shaking his head, he picked up a rag and started polishing the trim of his boat. Tomorrow would be better. He was heading out, like he'd planned before a particularly sexy woman had walked into his life. The Caribbean called to him—the wind, the sea, the freedom.

He tossed the rag back on the deck. "Damn!" Without Jessie, even the water had lost its appeal.

He'd thought about going to see her at least a million times. Once he'd even gotten as far as Nicole's street. He'd parked halfway down the block and sat, hoping to catch sight of her. But he hadn't gone in, hadn't called. He understood how these things worked, how a woman could think she cared for a man during a stressful situation. He didn't need her to tell him about it. He couldn't listen to her explain how she wanted to get on with her "real" life. So he'd stayed away, not giving either one of them a chance.

Of course, that was the piece that ate at him: he hadn't given Jessie a chance. He'd discovered a special woman, with a strength and capacity for caring beyond anything he'd ever hoped to find. And he'd made her decision for her.

"Damn!" he said again.

He might be an idiot, but he had to see her. He was going to make her tell him that she didn't care. That it had all been a lie.

Below deck, he took a few extra minutes to get cleaned up. He figured if he was going down in flames, he would at least look decent doing it. When he got back on deck, however, a small, dark-haired woman stood on the dock next to his boat. He looked up at her, squinting into the sun.

"You're not an easy man to find," she said in a voice that sent shivers down his spine.

For a moment he thought he was hallucinating. Then his heart picked up its pace, telling him otherwise. "I like it that way."

"You are Sam Cooper," she said, folding her arms below the sweet swell of her breasts. "The private investigator."

He held up a hand, offering to help her on board, amazed that she would really come to him. "Well, that depends."

She took his hand and stepped down. "On what?

"On who's asking."

"Just a woman," Jessie answered in her sexiest purr. "Someone looking for a hero."

He laughed shortly and captured her face with his hands. "Oh, you're more than just a woman. But me? I'm nobody's hero."

She slipped her arms around his neck and settled the soft length of her body against his. "Are you sure about that?" Standing on tiptoes, she nipped at his mouth, sending waves of heat straight to his groin. "Because I sure could use one right about now."

"I tell you what." He slipped his hands down to her waist. "Why don't we go below and discuss this? Maybe I can find you a hero."

"It has to be the right one."

. He worked his hands down to her bottom and pulled her closer. It felt so good to hold her again, to have her near. "Yeah? Why?"

"I'm afraid I'm hopelessly in love." Again she nipped at his mouth. "And . . ." Her voice faltered, as if she was suddenly uncertain. Then she said, "I think he loves me, too."

For a moment, Cooper couldn't speak. Instead he searched her dark eyes for the truth, almost afraid to believe. But what he saw left no doubt. Lowering his head, he gave her a long, searing kiss. Then he whispered against her mouth, "I think you're right. He loves you, too."

Weddings by DeWilde

Since the turn of the century the elegant and fashionable DeWilde stores have helped brides around the world turn the fantasy of their "Special Day" into reality. But now the store and three generations of family are torn apart by the divorce of Grace and Jeffrey DeWilde. As family members face new challenges and loves—and a long-secret mystery—the lives of Grace and Jeffrey intermingle with store employees, friends and relatives in this fast-paced, glamorous, internationally set series. For weddings and romance, glamour and fun-filled entertainment, enter the world of DeWilde...

Twelve remarkable books, coming to you once a month, beginning in April 1996.

Weddings by DeWilde begins with
Shattered Vows
by Jasmine Cresswell.

Here's a preview!

"SPEND THE NIGHT with me, Lianne."

No softening lies, no beguiling promises, just the curt offer of a night of sex. She closed her eyes, shutting out temptation. She had never expected to feel this sort of relentless drive for sexual fulfillment, so she had no mechanisms in place for coping with it. "No." The one-word denial was all she could manage to articulate.

His grip on her arms tightened as if he might refuse to accept her answer. Shockingly, she wished for a split second that he would ignore her rejection and simply bundle her into the car and drive her straight to his flat, refusing to take no for an answer. All the pleasures of mindless sex, with none of the responsibility. For a couple of seconds he neither moved nor spoke. Then he released her, turning abruptly to open the door on the passenger side of his Jaguar. "I'll drive you home," he said, his voice hard and flat. "Get in."

The traffic was heavy, and the rain started again as an annoying drizzle that distorted depth perception made driving difficult, but Lianne didn't fool herself that the silence inside the car was caused by the driving conditions. The air around them crackled and sparked with their thwarted desire. Her body was still on fire. Why didn't Gabe say something? she thought, feeling aggrieved.

Perhaps because he was finding it as difficult as she was to think of something appropriate to say. He was thirty years old, long past the stage of needing to bed a woman just so he could record another sexual conquest in his little black book. He'd spent five months dating Julia, which suggested he was a man who valued friendship as an element in his relationships with women. Since he didn't seem to like her very much, he was probably as embarrassed as she was by the stupid, inexplicable intensity of their physical response to each other.

"Maybe we should just set aside a weekend to have wild, uninterrupted sex," she said, thinking aloud. "Maybe that way we'd get whatever it is we feel for each other out of our systems and be able to move on with the rest of our lives."

His mouth quirked into a rueful smile. "Isn't that supposed to be my line?"

"Why? Because you're the man? Are you sexist enough to believe that women don't have sexual urges? I'm just as aware of what's going on between us as you are, Gabe. Am I supposed to pretend I haven't noticed that we practically ignite whenever we touch? And that we have nothing much in common except mutual lust—and a good friend we betrayed?"

Women throughout time have
lost their hearts to:

Starting in January 1996, Harlequin Temptation
will introduce you to five irresistible, sexy rogues.
Rogues who have carved out their place in history,
but whose true destinies lie in the arms of
contemporary women.

#569 *The Cowboy*, Kristine Rolofson
(January 1996)

#577 *The Pirate*, Kate Hoffmann
(March 1996)

#585 *The Outlaw*, JoAnn Ross
(May 1996)

#593 *The Knight*, Sandy Steen
(July 1996)

#601 *The Highwayman*, Madeline Harper
(September 1996)

Dangerous to love, impossible to resist!

RAC

MILLION DOLLAR SWEEPSTAKES

The Wrong Bed! The Wrong Man!
The Ultimate Disaster!

Christina Cavanaugh was *supposed* to be on her honeymoon. Except the wedding got temporarily canceled, their flight was delayed while the luggage went to Europe—and the bridal suite was flooded!

Hours later a frazzled, confused Christina crept into her fiancé's bed. But it was the wrong bed... containing the wrong man. And when she discovered the shocking truth it was too late!

Enjoy honeymoon bedlam and bliss in:

#587 HONEYMOON WITH A STRANGER
by Janice Kaiser

Available in May wherever Harlequin books are sold.

BRIDE'S BAY RESORT

UNLOCK THE DOOR TO GREAT ROMANCE AT BRIDE'S BAY RESORT

Join Harlequin's new across-the-lines series, set in an exclusive hotel on an island off the coast of South Carolina.

Seven of your favorite authors will bring you exciting stories about fascinating heroes and heroines discovering love at Bride's Bay Resort.

Look for these fabulous stories coming to a store near you beginning in January 1996.

Visit Bride's Bay Resort each month wherever Harlequin books are sold.

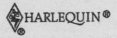

HARLEQUIN ®

BBAYG